in his own words

Paul Weller

Michael Heatley

OMNIBUS PRESS
London / New York / Sydney

Edited by Chris Charlesworth.
Cover & book designed by Michael Bell Design.
Picture research by Nikki Russell.

ISBN 0.7119.6097.6
Order No. OP47855

Exclusive Distributors:
Book Sales Limited
8/9 Frith Street,
London W1V 5TZ, UK.

Music Sales Corporation
257 Park Avenue South,
New York, NY 10010, USA.

Music Sales Pty Limited
120 Rothschild Avenue, Rosebery,
NSW 2018, Australia.

To the Music Trade only:
Music Sales Limited
8/9, Frith Street,
London W1V 5TZ, UK.

Photo credits: Front cover: Andrew Catlin/LFI;
Aki/Retna: 13; All Action: 80; Alpha: 46; Peter Anderson/SIN:
25b,44; Ray Burmiston/Retna: 84; David Corio/ SIN: 30b;
Kevin Cummins/Retna: 25t; Ian Dickson/Redferns: 6,36,40;
Erica Echenberg/Redferns: 9,15,58,69,81;
Martin Goodacre/SIN: 96; Harry Goodwin: 8,12b,91t;
London Features International: back cover insets,14,16,18,
19t&b,20,22,23,26,27,28,30t,31,32,33t&b,34,35,37,42,
43,47,48,50,51,53,54,56,60,62,64,67,68,71,72,74,77t&b,78,
83,85,87t&b, 89t&b,91b,92,93t&b,94; Neil Matthews/Retna: 76;
Suzan Moore/All Action: 39; Steve Pyke/Retna: 4,65;
Steve Rapport/Retna: 29,75; Brian Rasic: 88; Rex Features:
10,12t,21; Ebet Roberts/Redferns: 82; Ed Sirrs /Retna: 49;
Ray Stevenson/Retna: 7; Justin Thomas/All Action: 90;
Kim Tonelli/SIN: 52,55; Virginia Turbett/SIN: 24,38,41,61;
Chris Walter: 86.

Every effort has been made to trace the copyright holders of
the photographs in this book but one or two were unreachable.
We would be grateful if the photographers concerned would
contact us.

Printed in the United Kingdom by Scotprint Limited,
Musselburgh, Edinburgh.

A catalogue record for this book is available from the British Library.

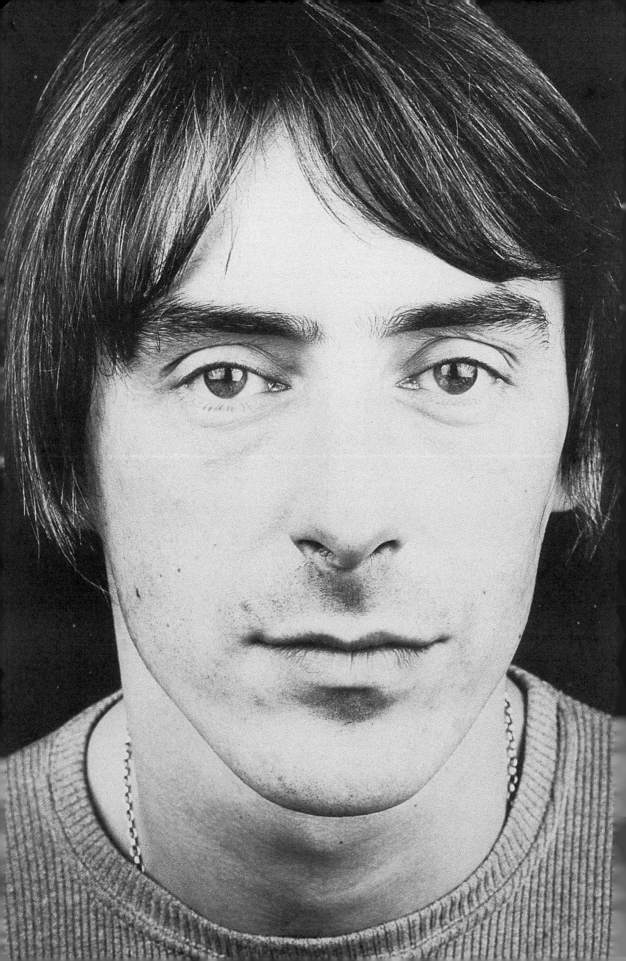

Introduction

It may be hard for long-time fans to believe, but 1997 is the 20th anniversary of Paul Weller's appearance on record. The single was 'In The City', the three-piece power-pop trio he fronted was The Jam. At first, there was little to mark them out in a hit parade dotted with new names and exciting music: besides, their early homage to the mod movement of the 1960s – sharp suits, scooters, Union Jacks and the like – suggested they might have a shorter shelf-life than most despite the obvious attractions of their melodic, energetic music.

Yet in The Jam's seven-year lifetime Weller developed their musical horizons far beyond those of mere Who copyists. He then split the band at their peak to pursue a completely different direction with the jazz-influenced Style Council, losing some fans but winning admiration from others: this was a man prepared to take chances. Then, after his record company rejected his first solo efforts, he returned from the wilderness as a figurehead of the new Nineties guitar-rock. Former fans like Oasis and Ocean Colour Scene (two of whom played in his band) now name-checked Weller in interviews and reflected his influence in their own music, capping an extraordinary rock renaissance.

With his sell-by date clearly still beyond the horizon, Paul Weller is one of today's most respected names. This book contains 'Wellerisms' from the 1970s, 1980s and 1990s as the Jam's angry young man turns into today's icon.

When You're Young

Early Days

Our family was always tight-knit. My Mum and Dad both had funny childhoods, they never got on with their parents, so they put a lot of time into me and my older sister Nicky. We were a very insular family. Just us against the world. *1995*

Woking used to look like villages, but now it's just offices. It's not a town any more, it's a commuter point. That's why most of it's car parks. *1984*

It's flattened now, the house is gone (Stanley Road in Woking where Paul grew up). I drove down there the other day with my son to go swimming, pointing out that I used to live there. There's a working men's club around the corner where I did my first gig. He wasn't interested. It's funny to look at those places, everywhere looks tiny and run down. All the reasons I wanted to get the fuck out of there.
  I've still got family there, but my main link with Woking is the area where I used to play as a kid, the woods around there, the rural side. The actual town's a dump, like most satellite towns. They've got a big shopping mall but no-one's got any bread and the shops are empty. *1995*

One side's all empty, rubble, and the other side's this big horrible red-bricked office block, probably been standing empty for 10 years. By the road sign there's a zebra crossing and I thought of walking across it barefoot, in a black suit, but I was talked out of it. It was a bad idea. *1995*

London was a special day out, you'd only go a couple of times
a year, which made it even more magical. Later on I came up to see
the Pistols at the 100 Club, that two-day festival with The Clash,
and then the Lyceum all-nighter, with Supercharge. That was it for
me: I've got to be part of this. It was happening, after a town
like Woking. People have a chance to be themselves in London.
In Woking if you had the wrong cut trousers you'd get your head
kicked in. *1995*

I had the idea (of becoming a pop star) when I was nine or 10,
around '68. I got my first guitar when I was 12. My parents were
cool, they always encouraged me. Took me about two years to learn
it. I did my first gig when I was 14 at the working men's club,
did a 20-minute set of covers, Chuck Berry and stuff. We did a pub a
couple of weeks later, just me and this other guy playing guitars in
matching shirts and loons. We did our 20-minute set and the old man
was going, 'Do it again!' So we did the same set again.

*Weller with Rick Buckler (centre)
and Bruce Foxton (right)*

Paolo (Hewitt, music journalist and friend) was asking me last night, 'What d'you think you would have done if you hadn't made it?' But I would just be in Woking playing the same pubs and clubs. Made the top of the circuit making the maximum money you can earn on that scene. I wouldn't have done anything else. There was no other option, like if this doesn't work maybe I'll do this or I'll try that. It wasn't even a case of whether I was gonna succeed or not. My success has surpassed anything I ever thought, but I always knew I would just do music at whatever level I got to. *1995*

I was making good money. We'd play two gigs a week. We did this same night-club in Woking for two or three years, every fucking Friday. Then Saturday we'd do a social club somewhere, so maybe I'd cop 15 or 20 quid, which at that time for a 16-year-old was enough. I can always make my living by playing music, whether it's big money or little money. That's my job, proper or not. I've done my apprenticeship and my college, and that was all those shithole clubs, playing between the bingo and the seafood. You know what I'm saying? *1995*

I missed the skinhead thing, but that was the first time I listened to black music in a big way (as a suedehead). At the dance on Thursdays it was reggae or Motown, Chairmen Of The Board, 'Sex Machine'. If you were a skinhead or a suedehead you listened to soul or reggae, while all the people with greatcoats, army bags and long hair had a copy of 'Dark Side Of The Moon' or Led Zeppelin. But I never liked any of it. Meanwhile we were doing R&B or rock'n'roll covers, mainly from my mum and dad's records, learning anything with three chords. Chuck Berry, Little Richard, Coasters. *1995*

Absolute Beginners

First Influences

My first musical memory? The Beatles. It must have been the
Royal Command, '64 or so. My mum would buy Beatle records and
take me to see Elvis films. My mum was young, she had me when
she was 18, so she'd be buying singles. But it was The Beatles
for me, especially from about '67, 'Strawberry Fields', 'Penny Lane',
the 'Mystery Tour'. Even up to '73, '74, a good few years after
they split I'd still buy their solo albums religiously. Even Ringo's.
Even 'Sentimental Journey', that's how dedicated I was. I remember
I was in the newsagents the day they split up, April 1970, I was
just devastated – 'I can't believe this'.

I don't like the three-minute pop song as in the sort of crap
you get in the charts, but I like the idea of just three-minute simple
stuff. I like all the soul of Motown and Stax – and the English stuff like
The Kinks and The Who and The Small Faces, all the bands that I
really like were happening then. Maybe that's stayed with me
because in my teenage years I never turned on to all that glam rock
stuff. I thought it was really boring, all that music in the Seventies.
So I suppose 'till I saw the Pistols I just kept listening to all them old
records. *1982*

When we first started the main thing we wanted to do was
become rich and successful. There was no musical movement that
had the same ideals as punk at the time, nothing that had dismissed
that way of thinking. However clichéd this may sound, it's true. It was
punk that changed my ideas a lot. Well... totally. I realised that the
music was more important. *1981*

I was always out to emulate all my heroes, Lennon, Steve Marriott,
Townshend. Their music, their clothes, their moves. Some of my
songs have been out and out copies, but I wasn't expecting anyone
not to notice. *1995*

Someone was asking me about authors the other day and I
said to them, 'Lennon and McCartney', because that's what I was
reading at eight years old. It was valid to me then and it still
is now. *1995*

Regardless of whether or not it shows in the music, my favourite
form of music is still soul. *1981*

When I was a kid The Beatles were the original inspiration which
got me involved with music. The Kinks were heroes too, but mainly
it was soul that I listened to. In '74 or '75 I got hold of a copy of
The Who's first album, 'My Generation', and the actual guitar sound

Left: The Beatles in 1967.

Above: The Who in 1965.
Below: John Lennon in 1965.

itself was so different after all that bland shit of the early Seventies which had no style, no look, nothing. So that's what influenced me, and that's why I copied The Who.

I loved The Sex Pistols, but the other stuff I heard in the Seventies, glam rock and all that shit, Led Zeppelin, Philly, none of it had any image. Now it's probably gone too much the other way, it's all pre-packed now, you can buy the image, the attitude, and all the rest of it. It's getting too easy and there's no challenge in it any more for people. There's still a lot of good music coming out of it, though, I like The Beat, Madness, The Slits, Department S, TV 21, but mostly it's individual records that I like. *1981*

I was a Beatles maniac from about '64 onwards, after 'She Loves You' and 'I Want To Hold Your Hand'. My Mum was only 18 when she had me, so she must have only been in her early Twenties at that time, and I remember her playing them and The Four Tops. I was really biased with The Beatles – I didn't care what it was, I liked it anyway. My uncle was a big Stones fan and he was always taking the piss out of me. *1992*

What's more important than anything is that The Beatles made me think, 'This is what I want to do'. *1992*

It was singles for me. At that time I was listening to Chuck Berry and a little bit of blues stuff... The Beatles, Little Richard. It was unfashionable but that was the appeal, it was different. Most of the kids were into Bowie or Roxy Music, that scene anyway, while the others were into serious progressive music... Things changed quickly though, they probably still do, but one minute everyone was a skinhead or suedehead, two months later it would all change and people would start growing their hair long. *1992*

Hopefully being moved by music is a process that will always happen – the day you don't get inspired by something is when you know it's all over. *1992*

When I was 16 I used to think I sounded like Otis Redding when I played my crappy demo tapes back. And I sometimes still think I sound like him. I've wanted to sound, at different times, like Marriott and Lennon, though I don't suppose I've sounded like either of them. But in my mind perhaps I did. When I was younger I was very, very impressionable. I'd get into a different artist every few months and play them non-stop, day in, day out. *1993*

When I was a kid and had just started playing guitar, all I wanted to be was in a pop group, be successful and make records. And I don't see anything wrong in that. I just got side-tracked. *1993*

I've got tapes at home, which I picked up in the States, of Beatles demos and John Lennon playing 'Strawberry Fields Forever' for the first time on an acoustic guitar. You can tell he's only just written it because he keeps hesitating over the chord changes and getting embarrassed about it. That sort of thing is wonderful, 'cos you get so used to the excellence of the finished product that you forget where it all came from.

If somebody told me there was an album out with some Small Faces or Kinks tracks on it I'd never heard, I'd go out and get it like a shot, however dodgy it might be. *1992*

'Strawberry Fields Forever' really caught my imagination – it's a very colourful record. I just thought the sound on it was fantastic and I couldn't understand how people had created it and that kind of intrigued me. It does the same thing for me no matter how many times I hear it. I wouldn't really attempt that sound. ELO had a pretty good run at it didn't they? But I wouldn't dare try to recreate it – no point. *1995*

For someone who used to have Beatle posters on his wall when he was a kid, thinking that years later I'd be working with the geezer (Paul McCartney), not only on a Beatles track, but in the same studio they all started off in… you can imagine. It took a while to get over it. *1995*

Did I have a favourite teacher? Yeah, there were four of them – The Beatles! *1996*

With Paul McCartney at the recording of the Help album for Brian Eno's War Child charity, 1995.

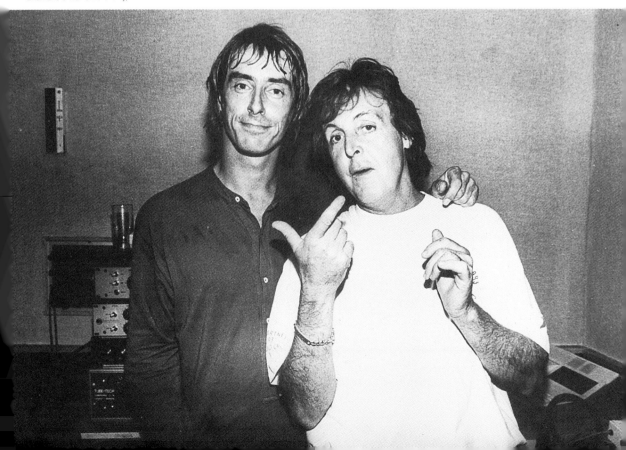

The Clash, c.1978.

Punks & Contemporaries

I find the music scene pretty boring at the moment... I'm fed up
with the three-chord bit. It's all a bit mindless. The Clash are one
of the most positive bands, and I still like The Pistols. The Clash really
have their set worked out. They're very professional, really creative,
but a lot of other groups are going to get stuck in a rut. *1977*

The punk scene was quite art-school and we were sort of ostracised.
It was quite cliquey and élitist in a London way. They were really
hip and we weren't, we were just three green kids from Woking, from
a little hick town and I guess our attitudes were like that as well. *1995*

(Punk fanzine) *Sniffin' Glue* wrote some review calling us retro.
Even then they were calling us retro. Bastards. *1995*

The really important thing about punk for us was that it connected
us into a contemporary scene for the first time. Before that, we didn't
really play to people our own age. *1994*

I either don't know who my contemporaries are, or they've vanished,
or I've got no respect or time for them anyway. I don't dislike Lydon
or Strummer. I don't really know either of them, but their music
doesn't do it for me. I don't want to slag them off because they were
a big influence on me at one time as well. But I don't really think
about contemporaries. I relate more to younger bands than I do to
my own peers. *1995*

People like Geldof, setting themselves up as spokesmen for the kids,
make me spew. *1977*

I wouldn't like to be going out on the stage singing 'When You're
Young' when I'm about fuckin' 30 or something. That's just a joke.
I don't know how some of these old groups have got the gall to do it.
They must either be stupid or really don't care.
    One of the biggest disappointments I ever had was in early 1978
when I saw (Clash guitarist) Mick Jones outside the Music Machine

with a bottle of whisky in his hand, staggering around. Someone
I really believed in hanging around with Mick Ronson and some old
rockers. *1982*

The whole thing about '76 and '77 has been totally romanticised.
There were only a couple of other bands who were worth anything,
and they turned out to be real wankers in the end. *1985*

I thought most of them (punks) were bullshitters. You'd see all
these groups playing pub gigs, with flares and long hair – and a few
weeks later, they were wearing skinny New Wave trousers.
There was a lot of that going on. And being 17 or 18, and being
arrogant, I thought I knew what it should have been about:
a real street movement, the first working-class musical movement
that our generation had had. We'd read all about the Sixties,
but it was the first time for us that something similar had happened.
That's what I wanted it to be. *1995*

I liked the attitude of punk but I also thought a lot of it was
fake. We all saved up about 20 quid to go to McLaren's shop – was
it called Sex at that time? – and we went in to buy some mohair
jumpers and found we couldn't afford anything. We thought, 'This
is bullshit'. At the same time what I got from those bands as a punter
was good, because it inspired me. Especially The Clash's lyrics –
some of those early Jam songs were awful, my attempts at being
socially aware, but that was me just aping The Clash, after reading
interviews with Joe Strummer and Mick Jones, saying people should
be writing about what's happening today. I'd never even thought
of it before. I was busy re-writing 'My Generation'. *1995*

This new sort of punk feeling that's coming back, all the new
punk bands, it's just fucking reactionary. It's like, 'We're going back
to the grass roots of punk, fuck this, fuck that, coppers are cunts.'
That is totally fucking irresponsible. It doesn't matter if it's created by
young kids or not, they should have more sense. *1981*

Well, you consider all the different bands and different types of
music in the charts. You've got like The Stray Cats, Spandau Ballet
and stuff, and it's all different styles. And not all of it is blatantly
commercial. If punk's done nothing else it's changed that, so that
any sort of music can get somewhere.
    I don't like the thought of The Jam when we're around 30
and old and embarrassing because I think we've always stood for
youth. *1982*

I couldn't understand that trendy side of it all, that college crowd.
I thought punk was the first working-class musical movement in my
time, that's how I perceived it. And I think that's why The Jam clicked.
We made our own scene. What we and our audiences were about
was more the real spirit of punk. Some of those groups were fucking
awful, don't you remember? The Cortinas… *1995*

The Man & His Bands

The Jam

Rock is supposed to be fun, something to dance to, to unwind you at the end of the day. *1977*

I've always said we're a pop band; I like pop music. I mean I've always said I like tunes and melody, so there's no compromise at all. *1977*

I've probably dropped a lot of the trendy ideas. Like everybody got caught up in the trendy political bit – I mean half of it was meant and half of it was just because everybody else was into it. So, I think I was probably a bit embarrassed of doing love songs and that, and now it doesn't bother me at all because I realise that love is an important part of people's lives – easily as important as politics. Our songs are more about people. *1977*

I thought 'In The City' was a great début album. It was rough, but that's how we were at the time. It was how it should be. Hopefully, in years to come it will be a well respected album. I'm sure when the second album comes out people are gonna say it's not as good. *1977*

I don't think they (Polydor) have sort of marketed us. People are going on about our image, but I don't think we've got an image. It's not a planned image. So, we wear suits, but we could wear anything. People create their own images. *1977*

We're the black sheep of the New Wave. *1977*

It's incredibly irritating to hear these bands playing stuff that means nothing to you if you're an 18-year-old. It's not just bands like Zeppelin. I mean, the worst thing of all is that disco shit. Disco's really fucked up a lot of music. *1977*

In 1974, Bruce Foxton joined us on rhythm guitar. Then this other geezer Steve (Brooks) left, Bruce and I swapped instruments and we became a three-piece band, more out of necessity than choice. Then we were playing local social and working men's clubs around Woking and Surrey, which was really boring but something we had to do. In retrospect it was good grounding for us. After that we started doing all the regular dates in London like the Greyhound, Hope & Anchor, Red Cow and the Nashville. We were given a residency at the Red Cow in '76 – or was it '77 – anyway, that was the springboard the band needed, and the crowds there got bigger by the week. *1981*

I don't think I'm very intelligent. My IQ's really dropped in the last year. I can't speak properly to people any more. *1978*

A lot of our songs have got humour in them that probably doesn't come out because people don't go into our songs, they just take them at face value. *1978*

I'm not preaching, but I'm trying to get across a non-violent stance. Street violence isn't necessary. *1978*

I ain't rock and roll. It's boring… leather jackets and greasy black hair, James Dean and motor bikes, all that rock and roll imagery is a crock of shit. Tony Parsons' book, the obituary of rock and roll, is no fuckin' revelation. Rock and roll's been dead for years. It died when Elvis went into the army. The Who never played rock'n'roll. They were an R&B band. They were soul, Tamla Motown. I don't think anyone's played real rock'n'roll for years. I think you've come to a point in time where you can't classify people like that. You can't put tags on people. Things are so diverse. *1979*

We're not a fun band. I don't like fun groups, groups that are just a good laugh like The Boomtown Rats. Without going over the top, it's important for a group to take themselves seriously. *1979*

It's difficult to be able to judge your own stuff, but I've got a fair idea of the standards we're setting ourselves. People say that I'm arrogant and bigheaded about everything that we do but it's not really true. I only like doing stuff that we think is really good. *1979*

Anyone who brings out that old Sixties revivalist tag now is an obvious arsehole. We're not reviving anything and we're as influenced by contemporary bands as much as anything else… probably more so than we'll admit. I still love all the Pistols singles. They are still one of my favourite ever groups. *1979*

I think we are a lot looser on stage now. On the 'Modern World' tour things were very clinical. But on this tour, there's a much better rapport between us and the audience. Our attitude has changed since the last tour. To me, it's more than just a group going out to sell their new LP. It's more of a show. *1979*

It's just impossible to do some songs live… for 'Fly' I'd have to change my guitar about three times. I wouldn't like to adapt my songs to that extent. Unless you can do something really well, it's not worth doing. A song like 'Life From A Window', without getting technical, has intricate acoustic and electric parts that would be lost live. I wouldn't want to spoil a song like that by doing it live. *1979*

A lot of the songs that didn't go on the 'All Mod Cons' album were fairly abstract. They were very weird, very diverse. A lot of the songs were written on the States tour and it shows! 'Sunday Morning' was

just totally weird. It was a really ridiculous country and western type tune, the sort of thing that Bert Weedon would do! 'I Want To Paint' was like this great fucking poem that was to be read out against the backing of a strummed A chord. Very weird stuff. That was during a period when I felt that I had to be sort of clever when I wrote, which is the wrong idea to have, really. There were some very pretentious songs, a lot of clever lyrics which would mean nothing to anyone. It wasn't really The Jam. It wasn't us… and we were thankful when the album was scrapped.

At that time we had simply lost all direction. I didn't really know what I was writing, and Bruce was off on his own tangent. One of his songs sounded like The Stranglers! I even played organ on it. We both know that the songs we were writing were shit, even though we got the usual buzz when we first went into the studio. It took a bit of time to realise that the songs just weren't up to what we were about. But if we hadn't been through that the third album would never have been as good. *1979*

'Billy Hunt' was written just after we got back from the States. It originally had a longer middle eight and a lot of the words were cut. I wrote it while I was still living in Woking, one day when I was sitting in the garden. I thought at the time that it had to be a single, but we held out until we had some other material. Polydor suggested that we waited until we had some other numbers. *1979*

The benefits of that period of slagging us off is just starting to show now. I think a lot of people fight better with their backs to the wall. When everything's going really groovy, you tend to just flow along with it. You're on top and you turn out a load of shit… which we have done at certain points of time. But I like having a bit of a contest. It helps me as a writer. *1979*

Signing to Polydor for £6,000 was something I was always really embarrassed about, which is a bit stupid when you think of it. The Clash signed for £120,000 and the Pistols signed for £40 million or whatever, so I was a bit embarrassed because it was almost like a credibility thing.

What is punk? We just play rock and roll, we always have done. It's only the press that have been bandwagoning the whole thing. *1977*

We wear that gear (black suits and ties) because we are really influenced by The Kinks, The Who and The Small Faces. In those early Sixties they wore this kind of gear. It's good. *1977*

In 10 years time I'd like to be living in the South of France. *1977*

You can programme a synth, press a button, and every time you know that note's gonna turn out perfect. Surely that's just as boring and indulgent as Genesis, Led Zeppelin and Pink Floyd who're always note for note perfect? I can't stand anything that's that perfect, to me once things get that good there's obviously something wrong. Our producer likes us to be note perfect, but rather than lose the feel I'd prefer to have something that's a bit rough but with some passion and soul in it. *1981*

Some people may learn music by reading and writing it, but I think that approach is a bit clinical, a bit soulless. The Jam, along with a lot of other bands, just seemed to develop. We never really had to practise to develop, it just seemed to happen. Even at sound checks we prefer to play something concise rather than just jamming away… far too boring. *1977*

I was more chuffed about finding my old Who badge that day than the record contract with Polydor. *1980*

There was a purpose behind going to gigs and I think in some ways that's been a bit sort of lost in the last two years. I don't really go out much any more, because it's just not the same. I don't feel that people are really there for the music. There's always that faction who are just there… all this sort of sectarianism, it wasn't there in the beginning. *1980*

When we first started people sorta looked down at us. It seems like people have gotta take notice now. We've sorta stayed there – we didn't sink without trace a year later. We've not only stayed there, we've also progressed. *1981*

I think that whole commercial sound has been made redundant anyway in the last two or three years. There's loads of good bands. The good thing now is that a song doesn't have to be immediately commercial anyway to be good or to be a single. 'Tube Station' I still think is the best single we've done, and it's not that commercial on first hearing. I think people are getting more into actually listening to the songs and that, not just the first hook line or something. *1981*

I really do feel we've never really captured our sound whatsoever, but I suppose in some ways it's quite inspiring. It leaves us something else to go for. *1981*

I'd hate us to end up old and embarrassing like so many others do. *(1982)*

When you go out to play a concert knowing that it's going through the motions, that's one of the most degrading things ever, y'know. It reaches a stage where you can't face the audience – can't look them in the eye. Those last few Jam gigs – it was like that. It was fuckin' awful. At that stage The Jam was so institutionalised, such big business. *1984*

I must admit this is the sort of LP ('The Jam's Greatest Hits') I hoped

Polydor would do one day. It's far more interesting to me than a bunch of A-sides stuck on a record. I think you'd have to know quite a lot about The Jam to be really interested in some of the stuff that's on it. But I could be wrong. *1992*

The Who's 'My Generation' was a massive influence obviously on The Jam… I've plagiarised the whole album, I think – I just changed the titles! We used to do 'Much Too Much' in our live set as well. This copy's signed by the Godfather himself, Pete Townshend. He must have only been 19 when he did this. Lyrically I think that it's really clever. *1992*

I believed then, as I believe now, that if a song still sounds good when you sit down and play it with just a voice and a guitar then you know you've got a good song. With 'Eton Rifles' I certainly did sit down and figure it all out before I played it to anyone. And I can understand how it might have been tough on Rick and Bruce when I presented them with a song like that and virtually told them what to play. It must have been especially frustrating for Bruce because he had such a distinctive style. But 'Eton Rifles' was an exception. Most of the time all I had were rough ideas and fragments, and we'd hammer them out together, with everybody contributing ideas. *1992*

'Setting Sons' was interesting because the arrangements, even on the early demos – just me on guitar – are almost exactly the same as they ended up on record. They're very complete songs. Then we just expanded with the bass and drums and a few overdubs or whatever. It's interesting to see how the songs built up. *1992*

I saw a ghost once in Italy. I was petrified… So I got up and wrote the third verse to 'The Bitterest Pill'. *1995*

I think bands have a tendency to give themselves all the credit for what goes onto a successful record, I know we did. It's only now that I realise we'd have been thrashing about in the wilderness if Vic (Smith, Jam co-producer) hadn't been there. *1992*

The guy who put it (the 'Extras' compilation) together, Dennis Munday, used to be our A&R man with The Jam, although he mainly worked with The Style Council. I thought it was a good idea and it's turned out as the best Jam compilation so far, the kind of album Polydor should be doing for the real Jam fan. Dennis had access to all the tapes – he dug out as many as he could find – and we compiled it between us, in that he'd send me cassettes and I'd say what I liked and didn't like. And he'd do the same. It was planned as an 'Oddities' or 'Rarities' set. There were so many B-sides that weren't on albums and then the other demos and unreleased stuff are obviously of interest.

Some of the unreleased stuff's good, although I wouldn't say there are any unheard classics – no singles, although there's perhaps one that could have been. So it covers early and late material, although everything is from '79 onwards. Anything earlier has either been lost or nicked, I guess! *1992*

We were never accepted. We were always a little outside of the whole punk circle which was quite élitist, cliquey and art school. Not Rotten, I think he's genuine, but the people who used to hang around that scene. They were mostly middle-class kids with rich parents, and they'd run away to join the circus. We weren't hip at all. We came from Woking, for a start. We saw things differently. *1995*

In terms of fun the early days were the best, travelling up the A3 in a borrowed Transit. There was no pressure because in our youthful arrogance, we thought we were gonna make it anyway, so we didn't give a fuck. The time I thought we'd really made it was when we did a four-week residency at this pub the Red Cow in Hammersmith. The first week there was 50 people there, the second week 100 people, by the fourth week it was queues around the block. The management came up to our dressing room and chucked in a free crate of lager. I thought: We're taking off. That was an exciting time and you only get that once in your life. *1995*

The End Of The Jam

I think it was quite a hard decision. It was the thought of us
continuing that I found more frightening…

One way I feel about it is we fuckin' meant it, and a lot of other
bands don't. I just think that if there's any kind of significance, it's just
that we're one of the first groups to ever do that. I always thought
that The Jam went a little bit beyond just being a group and just
being music. I think there's certain qualities about what we've done
that people could use in their lives. Some of my friends had some
good ideas. At the end of the gig, we should all go to the beach.
You know, the end of Quadrophenia, and he drives along the cliff on
his scooter? Sort of go down there and jump off with all our
equipment. I quite like that idea. *1982*

The longer a group continues, the more frightening the thought of
ever ending it becomes – that is why so many of them carry on until
they become meaningless. *1982*

How would I like The Jam to be remembered? I like to think that
we've done it more honestly than anyone before. And I'd like to see
young groups on the way up – and this is probably going to sound
really pompous – to be able to use The Jam as a guideline. To look
to us and think, well that's the way to do it. *1982*

I only listen to The Jam if it comes up on the radio or something and
it sounds really dated now, I think. It sounds sort of funny. I don't get
nostalgic for that at all. I don't think about it and I don't talk
about it. *1988*

It's sad, but as you drift apart you lose contact with people.
I haven't seen Rick or Bruce for some time. You move in different
circles – you make new friends. It's just a fact of life. *1992*

I wouldn't even slag 'em off (Bruce Foxton and Rick Buckler).
I really just don't care. Time was when we were all offered big money
to reform the band, but I would have needed to be really desperate
to do that. We had some good times, but it's never the same the
second time. I can see why some people do it – if Madness needed
the bread, or whatever. I don't begrudge anyone their living, but
imagine if, 12 years after The Jam, I was still doing the same thing
with Rickenbackers, still doing it on stage? Wouldn't that be fucking
sad? And wouldn't I be criticised for it? *1994*

I'm quite impulsive, but I'd thought about this (splitting the group)
for months and my mind was made up. People say it was selfish and
letting down the others and the fans, but it would have been more
of a let down to carry on just because we were earning good bread.
I've got nothing against earning good bread but I have to enjoy it
as well or it doesn't mean anything. I had a responsibility to the band

but we'd been together for 10 years – people forget that, because they only saw us for six. *1995*

He (Paul's father) wasn't pleased. We still had a contract to fulfil, some tours to do and some singles to make, and he talked me into seeing it through. But it was harder telling the others really, Rick and Bruce. They were gutted to say the least. Bruce was practically devastated. He didn't want to do the tour, he was so pissed off, so we were going to get Glen Matlock in – but Bruce came back when he heard about it.

It was a good tour as well. I think that freaked them out even more, the fact that I was enjoying it. We started putting a lot of the old stuff back in the set, like 'In The City' – for me it was more fun because there was less pressure. It's a hard thing to say when you've been with someone for 10 years, whether it's your missus or a group. You know – I gotta go. *1995*

They've (Bruce and Rick) been whinging in the press about how many Christmas cards can you send someone. I've seen that quote reprinted so many times, and their book came out, so they're obviously still bitter. But it doesn't make sense, 13 or 14 years after we split up. I don't understand it, to keep harping on about it after all that time, for Christ's sake. We formed the band when we were kids, made it beyond our wildest dreams, earned good bread out of it, had a good time, but all good things come to an end. I admire people like the Stones for keeping it together, but I personally couldn't do it. I like to move on. *1995*

Right from the time The Jam split, to be honest, I just felt that a weight had lifted. I know it sounds really corny but I did, and I don't think I ever was that miserable bastard that was portrayed. I know I have a reputation, but I get really bad depression now and again. That's just the way I am, not because I'm in a group, it's part of my personality – just like other people having corn flakes for breakfast. *1984*

Sometimes I look back on the old days and think, what a prat, but that's inevitable. I try to play those old Jam records, but I just can't do it. *1996*

The Style Council

A friend of mine thought of the name The Style Council. Somebody said they thought it was really pretentious but you can get lots of great puns out of it. *1983*

The name is misinterpreted. People just automatically think of clothes, whereas I don't. It wasn't really meant as talking about our clothes, it's more to do with individual expression: it's just a name… like Chairmen Of The Board. *1984*

It's a great name. I'll stand by that one. It was a snappy name, and I liked the disparity between the two words. *1993*

With Mick Talbot, Paul's partner in The Style Council.

I chose Mick (Talbot) for The Style Council because I wanted to have that organ sound, 'cos I still love The Small Faces and that whole sound, and Mick was the only young organ player who was still a mod. Most young keyboard players probably play synths now, they probably wouldn't think of playing an organ or a piano, but I just love the sound of both those instruments. The other thing was attitude. I didn't know Mick that well but he'd played with The Jam a few times and we found that we did have quite a lot in common.

   It was his attitudes. He was bored with the rock scene, he disliked all that macho thing and the drink and the drugs and all that shite. We were both more or less the same age, we both used to go to clubs at the same times and we both knew records from the early Seventies when we were both skinheads and suedeheads. It's just little things like that, things that would probably sound trivial to other people, but it's a mental thing when we're both clicking and both understand what we're on about. *1984*

People were down on it straightaway. And the more it seemed to annoy people, the more I liked it. I guess it was immature, but I used to like winding people up, I liked things that broke up the pattern of it all. *1995*

There are no wholly original influences really. For me originality just depends on how you interpret various styles. Jazz has been the most recent influence I suppose – Fifties stuff like Charlie Parker. The LP ('Cafe Bleu') simply reflects the diversity of The Style Council. In some ways, I don't think many people are going to like it. It's just not been made as a commercial LP. There are too many albums now that are just full of singles. I didn't want to make an LP like that. *1984*

I want to avoid regret really. That seems the worst thing to me. I don't really have that many ambitions really. I achieved most of those ambitions with The Jam. I just want to never have to look back with regret. With The Style Council there is no plan or direction. I'm pleased to have that freedom now. It's better that I have it now – better than if I had all that freedom when I was 18. *1984*

I think I appear a lot more human now. There was that horrible kind of 'seriousness' about me all the time before. Occasionally, I like to be a little pretentious these days, like on the 'A Paris' EP. Well, that was pretentious in a funny way. That kind of humour appeals to me. I like the 'pretentiousness' when somebody is aware of it. That can be very funny. But the inspiration for that record came from a lot of different ideas. Mainly though it was inspired by the Modern Jazz Quartet who have a lot of songs with European city titles.

I bought a lot of their LPs. Like their music a lot. The idea of those European titles seemed really pretentious. I thought I would use a bit of that. *1984*

Just because I'm not hammering at my Rickenbacker and my amp's not full up... people get the wrong idea. The intensity is there. If you listen to some of the early Temptations records – 'Papa Was A Rolling Stone' – well there's so much tension without all that power guitar. There's loads like that... Curtis Mayfield, Isaac Hayes, Bill Withers, Al Green. *1984*

He (Style Council partner Mick Talbot) doesn't think about things as constantly or as deeply as me. *(1984)*

After The Jam split I knew that I had enjoyed six years of commercial success. I recognised that I had no right to moan if I wasn't successful. I never am presumptuous about things. I was prepared to accept that the Style Council would maybe flop. Now that it's proved successful, it's confused me in a way. You always hope that it will keep going, I do mind about success. But perhaps it would shake things up if I released a single that totally flopped. *(1984)*

Well I talk a lot of shit a lot of the time and people should remember that. At the time of The Style Council I was just totally removed from everything, I was just generally much more judgmental. *1996*

'Money-Go-Round' is definitely one of the best things I've done. It's concise – I always like lyrics which are concise, compact. In some of the verses, each line is like a complete verse in itself. There's some really good slaggings of things in just one or two lines. It's kind of a potted history of capitalism – and all the offshoots of it. What I set out to do was just say what I think is wrong with capitalism. It's a bit historical as well. *1985*

Well, I've said a lot of things in my time and 90 per cent of them are bollocks, aren't they? But, yeah, I'm still anti-rock. That's an aspect of The Style Council I really like. To me, rock music – the whole sound and style and look of it – is a bit of an anachronism in this day and age. Yet it's still so popular. I can't work it out. It's weird to me. I don't understand what people like about it. I thought that punk was the last say on that in some ways. The Pistols were like the best rock band to me. *1988*

I don't think The Style Council audience is exactly the same (as The Jam's). There are still a lot of Jam fans and a lot of Paul Weller fans, people that like my songs and the way I write, but there are lots of people we've spoken to that never liked The Jam or weren't even aware of them but like The Style Council, so I think it's a mixture of those two.

Thinking about the last tour we did when we went on first and the support bands after and we did a second set – whether it worked or not I don't know, just doing that kind of show called for quite an open-minded audience, to get people to give it a chance, and I think that attitude amongst an audience is quite different. A lot of times a rock audience is very narrow-minded. I think of the stick the support bands used to get with The Jam and they never had a chance. *1984*

We have been pretentious but sometimes there's a purpose to it. Some of what people think is pretentious is just our personalised humour. I like that aspect of us – that the ideas are very insulated. There's a lot of depth to what we do. I think a lot of people miss some of the subtleties. *1988*

It's like a confessional. Miserable bastards? Yeah, I'd go along with that. It's fair enough, innit? *1988*

'Confessions Of A Pop Group' is just a kind of parody of a pop group like they've become now a commodity same as a packet of Daz or a tin of baked beans or anything else. There's lots of little threads. *1988*

'Life In A Top People's Health Farm' is about a lot of things, really. I just tried to cram as many of the tacky and distasteful things over the last few years into one song. I don't know if you can make the lyrics out on the track or not, but take my word for it, they're quite good. *1988*

In The Style Council I didn't have any confidence in my playing. I was totally bored with it and didn't know where else to take it. At the same time, I didn't know what else I was capable of. It took me a long time to get rid of a few hang-ups I had about my playing. I don't think I'm great by any stretch of the imagination, but I'm good and I'm getting somewhere with it, which is incentive in itself to play more. *1993*

There was so much politics and attitude that no-one talked about the music any more. Everyone stopped talking about it, including us, which was a very bad sign. *1993*

A lot of my audience who'd come with me in the first couple of years of the Council got pissed off with it. The media especially were down on me, though I can't say I had a rough ride because there were high points as well. But I thought we were quite misunderstood and misrepresented. Yet, at the end of the day, we made some good records and I wrote some good songs around that time, songs I still stand by, and I think that will last as well. Perhaps people will be able to reappraise some of them in 10 years time, or however long it takes for people's prejudices to clear. *1993*

We became incredibly arrogant, me and Mick Talbot, but mainly me because I directed things. *1993*

I like the songs on that (Style Council's Number 1 album, 'Our Favourite Shop'). We should have left it there. I lost interest after 'Favourite Shop'. *1995*

I hated all those groups who took themselves seriously. When I was wandering around when we made the Band Aid record at Island Studios… around that time, in the mid Eighties, everyone was so fucking full of themselves. The shittiest bands ever were this New Aristocracy. That's what I was against; it's what The Style Council were against.

People forget how many people were into the Council: the English press were down on it, but thousands of people came to the gigs and fucking loved it and still like Style Council records now. It wasn't like everyone was against us. We were big at one time, and I think we were quite influential as well, up until about 1985. *1995*

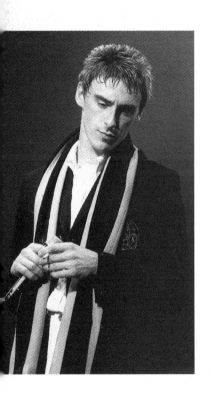

There were a lot of wind-ups with the Style Council that backfired. They were too insular. We found it funny but others didn't. We did this French EP, 'The Style Council A Paris', but the idea came from me getting into The Modern Jazz Quartet, doing 'Place Vendome', or Dexter Gordon, 'Our Man In Paris'. But unless people know that other stuff it's gonna look odd. Like The Modern Jazz Quartet wore these blazers with MJQ on them, so we got blazers with TSC on them. *1995*

My understanding of jazz is not because of musical proficiency, 'cos I don't understand those things. If someone plays a brilliant solo I don't know whether it's good or bad, the only criteria I've got is if it sounds any good to me. I don't know how good a musician you have to be to play (jazz), but if you have to be that good I don't see the point… *1984*

The original idea with the Council was to make an English R&B band, a modern Small Faces. And for me to stop playing Rickenbackers, to get a different sound and develop my voice. Miles Hunt was saying to me, 'How could you split a group like The Jam to form something as remote as The Style Council?' But why would I split one band to form another that sounds exactly the same? What would be the point?

I remember playing Rick Buckler some tracks off the first Style Council album, 'Cafe Bleu', before it came out. And he was stunned: 'Are you taking the piss?' I suppose it must have been the same for a lot of Jam fans. But I couldn't see the point in forming another three-piece power trio. *1995*

Sometimes it's good to have something to kick against, just as The Jam had been the black sheep of the punk fraternity. With The

With Dee C. Lee.

Style Council we were always intimidated in this country. A lot of our gigs here were pretty lame, but abroad we were really cooking sometimes. Here I had this constant baggage of The Jam I was carting around with me. It was as if there was nothing I could do to impress people in this country. We didn't have that anywhere else because The Jam never really made it anywhere else. We were fighting a losing battle here. *1995*

Towards the end of the Council I was disillusioned, I thought I'd lost the plot. I had no ideas what I was gonna do, and that's the only time I've ever thought about packing it all in. I was uninspired. I was writing but it wasn't what I wanted to hear. I was listening to garage, deep house, a lot of New Jersey stuff, groups like Blaze, though I missed out on the acid house thing. I liked the roughness of the deep soul stuff, like Willie Clayton, I was really into it. We made a whole album in this house style, which never got released. That was when we fell out with Polydor.

I think they should have put the record out. We were ahead in some ways. I thought it was the next development for The Style Council, the point being that we wouldn't just have the one sound. Good or not that was the idea behind the band. But people would have hated it, I guess. We did a couple of gigs around that time and

it baffled people. Weeks later I'd meet people on the street and they'd say, 'What the fuck was that about?' But I have to try. Whether it succeeds or fails I can't bring the same fucking record out for ever more. A lot of these acts now go away for four years and come back with the same fucking album. *1995*

We couldn't get along with the new Managing Director (of Polydor), a real bolshy fucker. I'm not used to people talking to me like that. Not because I think I'm Mister Superstar, but I'm not fucking having it. Basically because I am from Woking and I don't give a fuck, d'you know what I mean? So it was a personality clash and it was also over money. But I'm glad I got out, and now being with Go! Discs is like being with a real record company, with a bit of respect for the people on their label.
    To give you an example, when we had a play-back for 'Wild Wood' at the Manor, Andy (Macdonald, MD and founder of Go! Discs) shut up shop for the day, got a minibus and they all came down. It's that attitude. I walk in there sometimes and Andy is playing football in his office with a spliff on and a tape blasting. That's my kind of MD. You can even talk to him about music. *1995*

Sometimes I try and listen to some of those old Style Council records and they just sound really forced. I know it was a criticism at the time but they just sound really squashed in, like I was trying to find things but I just couldn't get there. It was my age, I think. In my teens everything felt like it was in black and white, and in my Twenties I think I just started experimenting, trying to find out about myself... *1996*

We're doing 'Man Of Great Promise' because it's a really good song and there's no reason why we shouldn't be able to play it. I mean, I fucking hated the Eighties, but now I can see that, however much we railed against it at the time, I was part of it, even though I never thought I was. The Style Council were an archetypally Eighties group without even wanting to be, but I was too concerned with the way things looked to see it. *1996*

Some of the line-ups... the one we had around the time of 'Cost Of Loving' was the fucking pits. But the one around '85 was hot. I was a lot different then. I remember around about the time of 'Favourite Shop', Mick had just had a kid, and I can see now the way that I was behaving toward him was ridiculous. I mean, I was a dickhead. But I always meant it at the time, though. Whatever I've done, I've always been totally into it. *1996*

I wouldn't say it was Mick (Talbot)'s fault, but I just wanted to finish the whole thing, go away for a while and think. It was strained, but we've worked together since then, he's played on this record ('Stanley Road') and 'Wild Wood', and we talk now and again. But it was quite ugly. We were trying to put this last record together and we were both uninspired, it seemed to drag on, and then, when it wasn't going to come out…

But it was the kind of jolt I needed, I guess. At the time it was very difficult, because for years I'd just been touring and making records and been successful. And for all that to suddenly stop was hard. Also I'd turned 30 around that time, me and Dee had our first kid around that time, those big changes in your life. I just stayed at home – I was a house husband. I looked after my son for a couple of years. *1995*

Solo

The music we play is really hard to define, there's lots of different strands in there. I'm really into a lot of things. I'm still listening to a lot of Sixties pop, just like I've always done. I'm also heavily into New York jazz-rap exponents Gang Starr, who are great, and I especially like the music being made by the British Talkin' Loud label. There's a band signed to the label called The Young Disciples who I think are excellent, and not just because Mick Talbot is their keyboard player! *1992*

Polydor made it clear they didn't want to deal with me any more, and the feeling on my part was entirely the same. You just go through 12 years of listening to people talking bollocks and you don't want to hear it any more. *1992*

I can't see myself ever moving back onto a major label. If I put any records out they'll more likely than not be released on my own independent Freedom High label. It's being proved nowadays that you no longer need major backing to achieve success. Bands like The Farm and The Inspiral Carpets have had massive success on indie labels, and with an indie you're free to do what you want. Thankfully there's no constraints of futile bullshit being talked. *1992*

I was very naive at that time (1982), and admittedly I made mistakes. Now If I ever did anything like Respond again I'd know how to handle myself. *1992*

I'm fortunate that I'm now in a position where I don't need to make lots of money any more. I'm financially stable but I still need to get out and play and write good songs. I'm still hungry! *1992*

I prefer those sounds (Traffic's 1968 album, 'Mr Fantasy') to the state-of-the-art digital sounds now, and consequently my records sound that way. I'm kind of a librarian of rock music, and those sounds are always on my mind. I'm always playing and thinking about the records from the mid-1960s onwards that I grew up with. But I'm always conscious of how people constantly hear these different references in my music, and whether, in a sense, they can hear me. I wouldn't just lift a sound; I see no point in that. *1993*

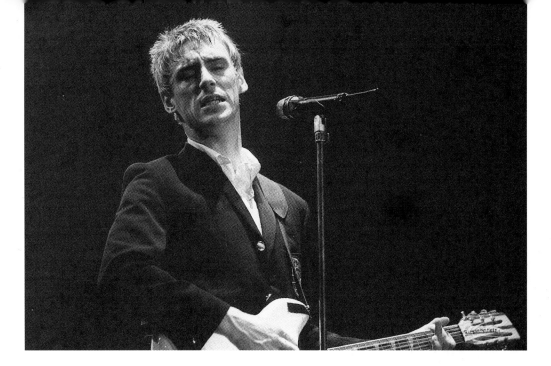

During parts of the Eighties I was so far up my own arse that I
wouldn't like to try to make any logical sense of things at that time.
People tried to talk me out of it, but I just fancied having my own
label. Who wouldn't? To do a label properly, you have to devote to it
as much time as you do your own work, or else something's going
to suffer, which it did. I got it wrong, and wouldn't do it again.
There you go. *1993*

What we were offered in England were insults. If I was 18 and
starting out, I might have accepted them, but in a country where
you're only as good as your last record, it looked like I might be
washed up. That's why I'm really pleased with 'Wild Wood's' success.
One, because I believe in the music, and two, because it's a big
'fuck off' to all the people who thought I was finished. *1994*

Never had a singing lesson. If I listen back to The Style Council,
it can sound very forced, like somebody trying to get somewhere
that isn't right. Music is psychological, so now I'm getting my chops
together, I'm not worrying 'does this sound wrong?' I don't care
about the odd bum note. *1994*

The Japanese are the only ones with the money who are willing
to part with it, and who aren't constantly on your back either, trying to
A&R you and rejecting your mixes. I'm too old to be bossed about by
some pimply-faced fucker. *1994*

That's the first ever take of 'Broken Stones' (from 'Stanley
Road'). We didn't even rehearse it. What you hear is the first time the
song had been played that way. It was one of those spontaneous
moments that only happen once or twice in a lifetime. I love the
images in that song. I was on a beach with my son when I wrote it.
He was asking me where all the pebbles were coming from. I told
him they were once part of the same big rock, but that time and the
waves and the weather had smashed it apart and sent different
bits all over the world. *1995*

If you're successful everyone's fine: 'Go and do whatever you want to do.' That's why this Brits stuff and all those awards are a loads of bollocks to me. Because four years ago I couldn't have got arrested. Now it's, 'Great, always liked your stuff!' That's the nature of the business and once you understand it you get on with it. It's quite simple. You can't trust it.

We use real instruments and don't make them sound hard and trebly like most sounds you hear these days. It's warm, and the bass will hit you in the gut like those old records did, before recording became technology-based or digital. *1995*

My idea for 'Wings Of Speed' (from 'Stanley Road'), was to fuse the feeling of an old English hymn with an American gospel sound. I can understand why some people might not like it, but even in The Jam I used to do ballads – 'English Rose', 'Monday', tunes like that. There's even a lot of little technical things – like certain chord changes or the way a verse goes into a chorus – that are still the same. It's just that the lyrics I write now happen to be a lot more personal. I tend to write them at night, when it feels like everyone else is asleep, but I never consciously decide what they're going to be about. It's just whatever bugs me most at the time, or whatever's on my mind. *1995*

Going back and listening to stuff I hadn't listened to for years, like The Small Faces, Sixties stuff, re-ignites a certain feeling, and reminds you what you used to get out of music. It also put me back in touch with my strengths, with what I'd forgotten I was good at, which is playing guitar. When I sing and play guitar it's a different thing. For a long time in the Council I stopped playing guitar, especially live. But there's definitely something about my songs when they're led by my voice and my guitar. They grab people, at least the people who are into what I'm doing. I guess that's what I was reminded of. *1995*

I still think 'Into Tomorrow' is a great record, and we just cut it in two days. In the Council, like most other people in the Eighties, we were caught up in technology, and most of our recording was done in the control room – fucking sequencers and drum machines – but 'Into Tomorrow' we just did over a Bank Holiday. *1995*

It did all seem to happen at once. I turned 30, didn't have a record contract, didn't have a publishing contract, had to sell our studio 'cos we couldn't afford to keep it up, me and Dee had just had our son... I felt awful for ages. I had no interest in music. I lost my direction, all my motivation, I kind of lost my bearings in it. *1995*

Every time you think you've got life sussed something else happens. And there's been quite a few things where I've just realised I know fuck all. I'm still starting really. *1993*

I would hope this LP ('Stanley Road') represents a significant change in me and my music. I've reached the bottom at times while also soaring to fantastic peaks (Glastonbury '94) and they both seem like scales out of control. I've tried to put some of those feelings into these songs. *1995*

I wrote 'Hung Up' down in Woking after Xmas '93 and almost in one day. I also started 'Time Passes' and I wrote another song called 'A Year Late'. I demoed all of them on the day after New Year at the Manor. We cut the master within a few weeks because it sounded so complete as a song, as is the melody, lyrics and arrangement, apart from one line in the middle eight section. But there you go – almost perfect. *1995*

I wanted to write a great English mod love song and 'Out Of The Sinking' is it. How did I feel when I wrote this? Frightened, insecure, crazy but powerful. It still makes my back tingle when I hear it. It still frightens me but in a wonderful way that I hope I can never explain. The middle section is pure Small Faces and proud, and the line 'Across the water' is the Thames. *1995*

On 'Wings Of Speed' I tried to describe the feelings I get from 'The Lady Of Shallot' by John Waterhouse which hangs in a bad spot in the Tate Gallery in London. Check it out. It's still free. I'm no art buff – I like what I like etc – but the lady in the painting looks real, she looks like she could step out of it at any moment. And the anguish in her face. The painting moves me and I don't really know why. I just enjoy it. I tried to make the song part Afro-American and part English hymn. *1995*

We had to get rid of Solid Bond (studios) around that time, which is the best thing we ever did because we'd have gone under otherwise. But things fell into place after 'Into Tomorrow'. I made the first album for this Japanese company Pony Canyon. The Japanese have the bucks. They haven't really got the handle on how you make music – these funny Western people make it and they'll pay you for it – but they were willing to part with dosh and let me get on with it, so the album came out of that. But we still didn't get a deal for a good four or five months in this country. *1995*

I knew I'd got my direction back, but 'Uh Huh Oh Yeh' was when I first realised I'd changed into who I am now, there's a lot in that song. I hadn't been back (to Woking) for about eight years, not since the Style Council started. And I only came back through here because I was going to buy a scooter in Aldershot. It's perfect, innit?
   Afterwards I drove back in the car and stopped off here, and went to a few places that I hadn't been to in years. And at the same time I started playing a few records that I used to listen to then – Stax, R&B, The Small Faces, The Who – and everything started to make some sense again. It just reminded me that that was what I was good at in the first place, y'know what I mean? And the funny thing

was, when I came back and I started doing those gigs as The Paul Weller Movement, well, there were only about a hundred or two hundred people at those gigs. It was all part of growing up I suppose, because if you don't laugh at yourself then maybe you never will... *1996*

'Stanley Road' is a culmination of all my solo stuff up to now. I feel like every track is complete on this album, d'you know what I mean? And that's a pretty dramatic thing to say really, because if that's the case, what's going to come after it? And I don't really want to have one of those albums, y'know? Because you've got to keep trying something new... Maybe it's just the first album in a really important stage. But I think it's definitely a step on. *1996*

I don't think 'Stanley Road' is an all-out rock album, but it is pretty intense. I hate going back to it all the time but it's all just down to the fact that we recorded the whole thing live, there were hardly more than two takes for any of the songs. And now and then it clicks and you get to that point where it becomes magic. Now, I know people have got to make out that music's more than that, but what it boils down to is playing well and writing good songs. It's a very basic, simple thing.

The thing about 'Stanley Road' – and it's not some sort of holy grail or anything – is just that it's got some real significance for me. I used to ask my old man how long a mile was, and he'd say, 'look down past the end of Stanley Road, and the length of the next road that leads off of it, and that's about a mile'. And I just remember looking down that road as a kid in the summer, and you know how the horizon sort of blurs in the sunlight, and it just looked as though it could go on forever.

It's to do with the family as well. Me and my dad often say to each other that it feels like a dream, the whole thing. That we'll wake up one morning and it'll never have happened. It's not like we've come from nothing, but we haven't come from anything special, we're just ordinary. And the best music always comes from that. 'In My Life', the Beatles song, that's the same sort of thing. Your roots are strong, and if ever you go away from them the pull's still strong. They're what keeps your belief going. *1996*

I thought 'Stanley Road' was complete, somewhere I'd have to move on from. But I've started writing new stuff and that's got a really different feeling to it. It's early days yet, though. When I say I'm writing, it just means I've got two verses or a great title or six chord changes I really like. But we've been listening to loads of old New Orleans records recently, like the Meters, Allen Toussaint, and Booker T & The MGs. I'm interested in that stuff because it sounds really dynamic, but at the same time there's still loads of space in it. Trouble is, I'd better not start talking about individual bands because everyone'll start saying: 'oh, it's heavily Meters-influenced', like the Nick Drake thing with 'Wild Wood'. And that's bollocks, man. It doesn't work like that. *1996*

That's Entertainment

Performing

Obviously if I didn't enjoy playing live I wouldn't be down here tonight, but I do prefer the studio. I think there's less limitations in the studio. But then again, there's limitations in everything. I just think you're less limited in the studio. *1977*

We want to work towards some slow numbers, but when the time is right. Not now. When I'm on stage for that hour or whatever, all I want is a speedy time. Whether that's a professional point of view or whatever, I dunno – it's just what I enjoy. When I see a band I just want to be kept up for that hour. And I think it's nice to have an album with a few songs that you don't play live. *1977*

I really hate rehearsing, it's the one thing that puts me off playing live, having to rehearse. It's bad enough having to rehearse one song, but rehearsing a whole set gives me nightmares. *1984*

They (festivals) are always full of bikers and their old ladies with their tits out. *1985*

I should be used to it by now (performing in Japan), because
it's such a different culture, but I can't thrash away on guitar all night
without any feedback. You think they don't like you, but they do
really. We had a riot once with The Style Council in 1984, but that was
very unusual. *1994*

I know I always go on about playing live, but it's the truth.
I've learnt a lot in the last few years, in terms of everything, but
musically I think I've finally come to terms with the way things should
sound. It's what I always talk about but it's the truth, all you need is
a decent band recorded live – you just have to be able to cut it.
The thing is, I still like playing music. I'm not good at being a
personality or a celebrity but when I'm on stage my ego gets what it
needs. That's when I'm at my best. *1996*

It has taken some time but now I understand what I'm good at:
that's playing live, conveying emotion, getting people fired up and
inspiring them. *1995*

When I'm on stage, it's almost like there's only one thing that matters: to prove my music, to prove myself. *1995*

It was frightening, the hysteria when The Jam were at their peak. I was very serious about what I was trying to say in the lyrics. The Jam would try and stay behind after gigs to meet people and break down this barrier, but it never worked that way. People still see you differently. I'd see people come into dressing rooms shaking. *1995*

I wouldn't do places like Wembley again, I hated it when we did it as The Style Council. You can't see anything and you can't hear anything. As a punter I've been to those gigs and the sound has been shit. So it doesn't appeal to me at all.

I'd play wine bars if I had to. It won't come to that, but I would. *1995*

Home & Abroad

Touring

It was painful (The Jam's recent UK tour), but that's just from
a selfish point of view because it was hard work. But I obviously
enjoyed it 'cos it was a major reaction. There's no way you can do a
different set every night, so we worked the numbers into a style
which highlighted each one best. *1977*

We're going to play there (the US) again, because there are
people there that want to see us, but The Jam are never going to
break there on a big level. None of the new English groups will.
Elvis Costello and Nick Lowe are the only types who could make it
in the States, not because they're bland but just because they're
more Americanised. But none of the other bands will because they're
all singing about Britain and it's very personal.

It's like us knocking The Eagles singing about California and
Sunset Strip because it doesn't mean anything to us. It's the same
to them – they don't know what Notting Hill or Wardour Street is.
It's worth going there to play to people who want to see you,
but some of the gigs we played we were regarded as a circus coming
into town. *1979*

I quite like staying at hotels for short periods of time – I like the rootless feeling – but after about two weeks it starts to do me in a bit and I need to return to base. My life's like a game of Monopoly really – I have to return to base every now and then and collect £200! I like being quite ordered in hotels: I lay all my clothes out, put my toothbrush out and stuff like that. I'm quite tidy as well. I'm not untidy in hotels because I think you've got to respect the maids. **1984**

Getting back out playing live was a really weird and at times nerve-wracking experience, although we had mixed press reviews, the tour was really therapeutic, and playing live sparked something in me. Maybe getting out there again made me realise just what I'd been missing. I think, with hindsight, that staying out of the limelight for the time I did – around two and a half years or more – was far too long a period to be away from it all. **1992.**

We went to America the first time and did the Whisky A Go Go eight nights in a row, 16 shows back-to-back. First show, they'd come off and they had them funny little suits then with the lapels and the funny button-down shirts, and they'd be soaking. I'd take 'em back to the hotel and tell the boys I was getting them dry-cleaned. Was I fuck! I put everything into the tumble drier, a bird in the hotel pressed 'em up and they went back on dry for the second show. Of course, they shrunk past the ankles eventually, looked funny, in fact, but you didn't care. You were out in America, California, Los Angeles. Fucking great! **1994**

I get bored if I stay in one place for too long. I couldn't travel for months without a break, like some bands but, for a few weeks at a time, I love it. It's great when there's a gig every night and we're all up the back of the bus, playing tapes really loud. That's proper touring. It's fun because everyone's together. Yesterday in Zurich, R.E.M. all turned up separately. They each had their own huge coach, with about two other people on it. All that proves is that it's time for them to quit. *1995*

I was away (as usual) on Natty's sixth birthday. We had started another US tour but I got to play 'Moon On Your Pyjamas' on the same day, live on New York radio. It's sentimental, yes, but I was trying to send out signals to my son, messages. *1995*

My Ever Changing Moods

Home Life

I believe in the family unit and all that stuff, and I'm also quite a loyal person, so if I've got friends I stick with them, I'm not fickle... *1984*

Quite a lot of people have felt detached from their parents whereas I've always been the opposite... we've always been friends. We always used to go out drinking when I was younger, Dad would take me and my sister out. I love my parents and I love my family so if we can work together as well that suits me. *1984*

I don't really need much sleep. If I do, I'll go to sleep wherever I am for an hour or so to refresh me. Sometimes, I'll go to bed and I'll get up around about three in the morning and write for a little while. I just write, I don't play any instruments at home because I don't like to make too much noise – I think the neighbours'll listen and think: 'Oh, there's that pop star writing his songs again.' I just find it inhibiting. Sometimes I have to force myself to sleep. It's so boring sleeping. You waste such a lot of time.

I'm a bit one-track minded I suppose. The last time I went to the cinema was about three months ago to see... what was it called... *Muriel's Wedding*. That was pretty good. The only books I've been reading have been music books, about those Delta blues musicians...

When I was in The Jam, I wrote about other people's feelings. Now I write about myself, my feelings, my emotions. I like the way music can get you through the dark periods. That's important. I had a time when I split from Dee a while back, and writing songs helped me out the other side. *1994*

I mainly just like listening to music. It still inspires me – I still get something from it, a very personal thing I can't put into words. It's the only thing that really excites me, to be honest. It worries me sometimes, because it does feel like I've got a very one-dimensional life. It all just seems to revolve around music. But that's the way it is, I've accepted it. *1995*

Fame and wealth hasn't made me unhappy but I'm never really totally satisfied with anything I do, whether it's records or whatever. There's always something else I want to do, I always feel I wanna do more. I suppose that keeps me going. I never get complacent. Owning six Rolls Royces, a mansion in the country and all that shit has never interested me. I try to live a comparatively normal life, which makes it easier to stay in touch with things. If you're interested

With wife Dee C. Lee and children Nat (7) and Leah (3) in Holland Park, London.

in life then it's easy to stay in touch. Mind you, I never seem to sit down and just enjoy it all, because there's always something else to do. *1981*

It's nice to see your kid grow up from this tiny thing to a little person. But I can't say I was happy as a person, because I was frustrated, away from the thing that I need, let alone love, which is to play music. *1995*

I feel pale in his (John Weller – his dad) shadow, a hard act to follow. Yet it's me who receives the accolades and applause. Hopefully he gets his through me but that I'll never know. *1995*

Nat (Paul's son)'s seven now, so he's well up on it. He's been to a couple of gigs. They're both aware of what their mum and dad do. They're proud of us. *1995*

I suppose when you're stoned you can really concentrate on things. Sometimes that can be to your detriment; you can watch a lampshade for 15 minutes and really understand it. But other times you'll be really good because you've got that focus. Having said that, my music isn't very mellow or laid-back. I think it has more effect on the way I listen to things. And you know, I made plenty of good records in the past without smoking dope. *1995*

You have to be practical with kids. You don't have time to sit around being analytical, because you've got to feed them or clean their arse because they've just shat themselves. I like that thing of being tapped into earth again. And, being separated from Dee, I miss that stability. *1995*

Am I a good father? Yeah, I think so. I was looking after the kids for about three weeks there and it was brilliant. They make me very happy. My daughter Leah is a real performer. She's not even four and already she's right into singing. She sounds like Hilda Ogden though, really high-pitched, but even more falsetto. And she's beautiful. Fortunately, she gets her looks from her mother.

   She'll definitely do something, either sing or play or dance. She's always doing it; she seems like a natural performer. She sings really well, and when she plays piano… she can't play properly, but she plays very daintily. Most kids just thump it. *1995*

Well, sometimes I feel more rounded for having kids, and sometimes I don't. I don't feel wholly secure now, even for all the success. It's just not in my nature. I'm always trying to prove myself. The point about having kids is that, before you know it, you just start worrying about them and their future. It's never-ending. *1996*

Sex & Relationships

I quite envy happy bisexuals. *1982*

Am I a flirt? No more than anyone else. I just like women.
There's nothing wrong with that. My perfect date? Raquel from
Coronation Street, probably. She's fuckin' alright. Am I a lad? No, I
don't think so. Well, maybe I am when I'm drinking. That's why
I'm off it at the moment. I do stupid things when I'm drunk, which
I really don't like. After a few too many, I have been known to pass
out in bars or puke up on people. It's good to wake up in the morning
and not feel like shit. *1995*

There were some pretty nice girls out there today. I saw at least
a couple in really cool tops. In the past year there's been a lot more
women at our gigs, which is great. The majority are still geezers,
though. I suppose it's due to the whole Jam legacy, which was
always very laddish. Why? Because it's quite brutal music, macho
maybe but not purposely so. *1995*

Paul's Philosophy

Positivity is what we believe in. Instead of fighting each other we
should fight for the basic things that matter. *1977*

The Arts Council are useless. Kids aren't into pinball machines and
coffee bars anymore. They should be shown that life doesn't revolve
around football matches and TV. They should be encouraged
spiritually, as well as financially. *1978*

I'm never really happy wherever I am. *1980*

You've got to retain some kind of optimism or else it's pointless.
However misplaced or naïve that sounds, you've got to retain some.
1981

People seem to be getting more and more closed-minded about
things. It's kind of a spiritual thing as well, do you know what I mean?
People don't seem to have that same sort of spirit inside them.
Or maybe they have but they're losing it more and more. *1981*

In the Western world, all your responsibilities are taken away
and done for you. It starts at school, like losing that individual spirit
and replacing it with a cosy environment where your only
responsibility is to get up every morning to go to work. *1981*

I like that George Orwell quote: 'If liberty means anything at all, it means the right to tell people what they don't want to hear'. *1982*

I like my Dad's attitude, always have done. He's never been conventional and that's why I like him. If he jacked it in, I would as well. Definitely. A lot of the times he's the one that's kept it going. *1982*

I'd like to be in things on TV. Like the end bit in Benny Hill, you know, the bit where they all chase each other round the park speeded up. *1982*

Play in front of anybody, your friends, your Mum and Dad, anything to get it out of the bedroom and gain a little self-confidence. Play along to records, don't waste time learning to read music. Forget all the rules, do whatever you think, do whatever sounds good to you. *1981*

I think it's good to encourage people – I know that sounds patronising but I think it's good to try and use as many as possible. We could use session singers; you know you'd get a good sound but I don't think you'd get a good feel. *1984*

I never wanted an office job! It just doesn't interest me. I'm just interested in the music and the records. *1984*

I don't really give a fuck any more about what anyone thinks of me. *1986*

I've always been a bit of a cynic and on matters of the human race I'm more and more cynical. But, I mean, I've still got a kind of hope for the world that at some point in time it'll see what's wrong with it and people will put it right – which is idealistic nonsense, really, especially in this era. *1988*

I find these days I'm more of a mind to say, Oh, sod it. I just think, 'Can't you see what's going on?'. I mean, I can understand the people who've got a vested interest, the moneyed classes, supporting Thatcher, but the working class just makes me despair. You think, 'What's the matter with all you working-class gits?'. Which is a little bit idealistic and a little bit naïve. So I suppose I am a naïve idealist. *1988*

A song can make you happy or make you sad. I think that's the most positive aspect of music. Who knows? *1988*

It was a bad time, a low time (1989). But I realise now you've got to go through it. Up until then I'd had quite a cushy ride, really, and now I'm prepared for whatever comes my way. It did me good, helped me come back down to earth a little bit. It made me doubt whether I was as strong as I thought I was. But it has turned round, though it's taken three years or so. The turning point for me was writing 'Into Tomorrow' on my first solo album. Up until then I thought I'd lost it. Sometimes you just have to wait until it comes round, which I'm prepared to do now if it happens. *1993*

I've dropped a lot of my musical prejudices. For a long period I wouldn't play any records by anyone who had long hair or a beard. Now I play anything good. That's one of my duties in life: to hear everything I can, open myself up to anything. I listened to Free's 'Fire And Water' album recently, and that sense of a really tight band playing together live is the kind of thing that really moves me a lot these days. *1993*

I hope for a coming together of people, a realisation that the world can't continue without us all co-operating and interacting. That we'll do away with the Houses of Parliament and turn it into an Arab hotel, and also turn the Dorchester into an NHS Hospital. For me, personally, I hope to get a great singer to cover my songs. *1994*

In a way, I've come full circle, because when I started out playing as a kid, doing the clubs and pubs as a semi-pro, all I cared about was music. It didn't take long for the other stuff to get in the way. I never thought I was qualified to be giving political opinions. I see it as a dangerous thing in people like Bono. All that rock star swaggering. What does that mean? But I wasn't ever a spokesman for my generation, either. That was something the media stuck on me. *1994*

Some people read. I'd rather put on a tape or record. I get the same nourishment – both mentally and physically – from music. Because if you take away the music, I don't know what else is left. Not an awful fucking lot to be honest. So I have to immerse myself in this. I don't know what else to do. *1994*

I didn't have anything to do with acid house at all. I never agree with any of that thing about taking gear affecting your music. I'm sure Coltrane and Charlie Parker would still have played great without drugs, but they'd have lived longer. I'm sure John Lennon would still have written 'Strawberry Fields' without acid. You're either an artist or you're not. *1995*

I've certainly started to see what really matters in life: my kids and my music, and that's it. I'm pretty down to earth at the moment. I think I've got my head screwed on. There have been times in my life that I've acted like a total prat – in The Jam, in The Style Council and fairly recently, I guess. To me, it's all just part of growing up. I can't say I'm always going to feel like this, or be this down to earth. I could have more phases of acting like a pop star along the way.

It is really easy to get caught up in your own ego. I mean, I've gone way past the stage of believing all the people who tell you that you're great. I got over all the crap years ago. Sometimes, though, I catch myself thinking that only what I'm feeling or seeing is important. Sure, everyone does that, but you get the chance to indulge it a lot more in music. It's true. You can behave terribly badly in this job and simply get away with it. *1995*

I get these insecurities, or a sense of failure, or the idea that I'm not living up to what I want to get to. And then other times, I walk off the stage at Phoenix or T In The Park and know exactly what I'm doing and why I'm here. *1995*

I don't believe in politics any more. I don't believe in religion particularly. But I am hungry to make music. It's like my faith, really. *1995*

I'm just a man, I can be a bastard like every other man. People see you on stage and they see you on TV, so they see you differently when they meet you. It's like with The Jam, we stayed behind for ages after almost every gig for years, an hour, sometimes two, longer, talking to people. No stars… It don't work out like that. I don't want to be put on a pedestal. I'm no different to anyone else. *1995*

I think E changes your attitude as to the way you interact with people and how you feel about yourself. It wouldn't influence me musically; my music goes on with or without taking gear. *1995*

When I was a kid and I listened to 'Strawberry Fields' I could never articulate what it meant to me, but it did mean something. The line 'No-one else is in my tree,' that was enough for me, that's how I felt as well. It's an arrogant statement but even as a kid it meant something. A lot of the new songs are really intense. It gets more complicated as you get older. What could be more complicated than coming to terms with your own mortality?

But the up side is I get more confident. You give less of a fuck if people don't like you. But things don't get easier. I personally couldn't be a pipe-and-slippers man sitting in front of the telly and being mellow. I want to know what life's got in store. *1995*

Celebrating his birthday with wife, Dee.

I haven't worked on my voice at all. I'm still smoking loads of ciggies and drinking, but it seems to be doing the trick. I'd recommend it. *1995*

When I look back on the last couple of years, it'll definitely be a golden period. Personally, things haven't gone quite so well, but I s'pose that's all part of the learning process. Somewhere along the way I've realised just what I'm good at, and that's just singing songs and playing the guitar. Playing live has been a real high this year, and splitting up with Dee has been the complete opposite. But these things work against each other. You've got to be philosophical about it… *1996*

The thing I don't understand is that a lot of bands don't seem to be doing it for the right reasons. For me, it's not about the money, it's about doing the best you can possibly do, and if you get money or success from it, it's irrelevant. I'm always thinking that I could do something better the next time around – and I don't care what people make of it, whether they think it's contrived or not. Of course it isn't.
  I remember when I was involved with Red Wedge and I'd be in all sorts of stupid situations, like when there was that board meeting we did with the Council for the *NME*. That was fucking ridiculous. I don't believe in religion or politics, just in music, pop culture. That's my religion, it's just what I do. *1996*

I can't see where things are gonna end. You can't put an age on it or anything as simplistic as that. And I'm sure that, if I was going to have some sort of revelation about why I'm doing this, or when I should stop doing it, it would have happened by now. Trouble is, there's hardly any examples of people who carry on and don't just become more and more showbiz and more and more boring. There's only Neil Young and Van Morrison. The thing is, I want to match that rawness they've got with the mood of songs I'm singing as well.
  It'd be easy for me to write an album full of songs about splitting up with the missus, but I don't want to do that. That's why I like that Supergrass tune, and something like 'Staying Out For The Summer' by Dodgy. Not so much for the tune but for the spirit of it. I'd like to make the next album with that sort of spirit in mind, a really happy record. *1996*

I only keep faith in music because that's the one thing that's stayed with me, that I can rely on. And that's just because I put so much time into it, I get the rewards back from it – if I wait around long enough... *1996*

Changing Man

Age In Rock

People under 20 are very different, they're fresher. They don't try and intellectualise music, they don't have that phoney pretence about it. They're more intuitive. *1983*

I've still got problems: we're just putting it over in a different way, that's all. I don't know whether I would have kept on doing it anyway because I wouldn't want to become like The Rolling Stones, I wouldn't like to be jumping up in the air with my guitar at 40, or even at 26. I think after five years' initial success, after the period of their best stuff, people stop being a group and they start being actors of what they were, just play the role of what they were at their peak.

   That's like trying to stay 19 until you're 38. That's one thing I've got against people like the Stones trying to emphasise the fact that they think they're still young rebels. I mean you just don't cut it, it just doesn't work, after a while you look stupid physically. *1984*

I don't want to mellow out. I'm just going to do what I want to do and say what I want to say. I don't care if people think I've cracked or whatever. I'm an angry young man!

Well, I started mellowing when I was 26 or something, didn't I? According to you journalists, I've been mellow for six years since I learned how to control feedback and stopped sweating on stage. I don't know if I've mellowed, really. I have in some ways and I haven't in others. It depends on your character, doesn't it? Maybe I've become more reasonable. I think this new LP ('Confessions Of A Pop Group') is quite angry in some ways, but I can't tell really. **1988**

Part of me gets very pissed off with it (crowd calls for Jam songs), but another part of me understands the reasons why. Let's face it, The Jam made a big impact on many people and I suppose it's only natural they'd want to relive a few memories. **1992**

There've been times I've been so arrogant I wouldn't listen to anyone anyway, but I reached a peak, and now I've come back down to earth. **1993**

Go and look back over 18 years yourself and see how you grow and develop: everyone does it. The only difference is that I've done it in public. **1995**

Now I'm gonna look after my own arse. That's how I feel. It's different when you're younger, forming a band, you all start off on the same footing, but it gets harder the older you get, the more history you gather, to be democratic. You're all growing different ways. You start off with a single idea, that we're gonna make it, but people change. I like the fact I'm not responsible to a band now. It suits me. **1995**

Things change, perspectives have to change really. Well they don't have to, but mine have fortunately. I still think I'm going through quite a transition at the moment. I don't think you ever stop changing or learning. I used to think that maybe things get simpler the older you got, but I don't know. **1995**

I don't know if I'm getting older, but no one seems to be able to sing any more. They talk sense, like that little bird from Echobelly, she was very nice – but then you see them perform... **1995**

'Into Tomorrow' is... about me trying to get a grip on becoming thirty something and the great grey mass that lies between the simple black and white world of my youth. **1995**

The Walls Come Tumbling Down

Politics

The Queen's the best diplomat we've got. She works harder than you or I do, or the rest of the country. I don't see any point in going against your country... that's not really a positive thought, is it? This change-the-world thing is becoming a bit too trendy, we'll be voting Conservative at the next election. *1977*

We don't love Parliament. We're not in love with Jimmy Callaghan, but I don't see any point in going up against your own country. If there is such a thing as democracy, then we've got it. *1977*

Things are always taken out of context, so I've given up talking about politics. Besides I don't see why anyone should be interested in my politics anyway. I don't make any startling remarks. It's not up to me to brainwash or influence anybody. If there's a message, it's in the songs. If people see the message and listen to it, then it's up to them, but I'm not gonna force anything on anybody. *1977*

I'm sick of everyone calling us conservatives and saying we're not radical enough. I think Jim Callaghan and Margaret Thatcher are cunts. I don't trust any of them. All I said at that time was that I thought the Tories would do less of a bad job... *1977*

Starving and Cuba and nuclear activity... it scares me sometimes, but I also think what the fuck can I do about it? The sheer fact that I put it down on plastic isn't going to change anything. I could put my feelings down on plastic and send it off to all the heads of state in the world and they're not going to hear it, and even if they did they wouldn't do anything about it. All you can do is operate within your own people. It's like a series of tribes or something, we're just operating within our tribe. *1979*

I said a lot of very naïve things last year. If anything I'm apolitical now, I'd vote for the Labour Party because that's the only way to keep the right-wing fascists out. *1978*

I never see life as being steady. I've always been uncertain. I've never felt I could sit back and relax there's just too much going on. I'm sitting there in front of the TV moaning on about world politics saying 'look at these bastards' and Gill just says 'yeah, shall we start tea then?' And she's quite right.

Maybe I'm only an armchair radical. But every night I watch the news and I get so frustrated. I write it all down, then in the morning throw it away because it's rubbish, just paranoid rantings and ravings. *1980*

The music industry isn't worried about politics. It doesn't affect them. Their only objective is to sell records, and it makes life easier for them if you're singing about girls and cars.

A pop song ain't exactly going to change the world but it can act as a vehicle for thoughts and carry those thoughts worldwide. *1981*

That rock rebellion thing is dead, it should be buried as well…
The real rebels are the people that are actually doing something: it's not group, it's not music, it's people like the women at Greenham. The CND marches, they're the people that are trying to do something about it and not just singing down a fucking microphone – and I'm not putting myself outside that, either. *1984*

It's important for kids to voice their dissent and try and do something about it. And things like *Smash Hits* should be helping. The thing is to get away from the point of view of 'well, *Smash Hits* is a pop mag so there's no room for politics'. You know, how can you disconnect the two? How can you disconnect politics from anything? *1985*

I'm proud to be working class but I want to work towards a time when I'm completely class-less. And everybody is. Even now, it's crazy. People still treat you as 'inferior' because you're working class. Money's got nothing to do with class anymore, and yet the rich – especially in this country – really parade their wealth. I find that astonishing. It's like, a few months back, there was this story in the papers about all these rich people flying all the way to the south of France for some stupid party and then flying all the way back on the same day or something stupid. And the papers made a really big thing about it. Splashed it all over the covers saying – in so many words – y'know: 'Isn't this great? Wallow around in all your poverty and then forget all about it by reading how the other half lives. Isn't it exciting?' I really hope the working class won't take that much longer. *1981*

Perhaps I'm interested in a more subtle form of attack these days. A lot of people remarked recently how 'mellow' I have become. I just find that really funny – it just seems that people don't look very far sometimes. Some people just don't listen.

  I'm not a card-carrying member of any political party and I have no intentions of becoming one. I don't think I've shied away from making statements this year. Did you hear 'Money-Go-Round'? Well if you can call that shying away? I thought it was very specific. I wouldn't want all my songs to be about political subjects because I don't live my life like that and I'm not a member of the SWP. That's not the way I work – I've got a mixture of feelings. *1984*

I thought about joining the Labour Party cause I thought I ought to. I gave them my vote at the last two elections. I would probably support them on most things. I just wouldn't like to give myself totally to one party though. There's always something that let's them down. It's like the SWP – they're against nuclear bombs but for IRA bombs. I'm against all bombs – I can't tell the difference; they all blow innocent people to fucking pieces. It's wrong. I can't completely commit myself. *1984*

If you ask us all questions, you'll get different answers. But we all want to get rid of the Tories. **On the launch of Red Wedge, 1986**

It's a bit pompous to think I could make a difference. Anyway, I don't believe that as much as I used to. Music doesn't overthrow governments or start a revolution, does it? I realise that. *1988*

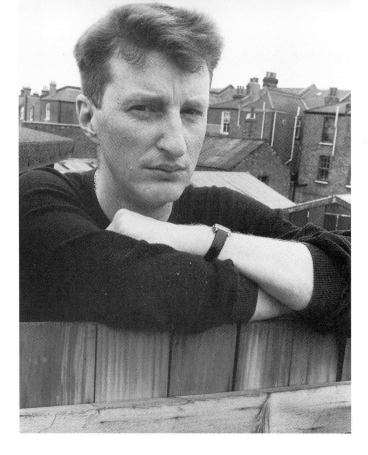

Right: Billy Bragg.

I don't like joining clubs: I like to feel part of the human race, but at the same time I'm a very individual, very private person. I don't like the idea of carrying a card. The Wedge thing (the so-called 'Red Wedge' 1985 Labour Party youth drive led by pop music) escalated from when a lot of artists, including us, were doing benefits and someone decided to pull it all together. I felt uneasy about getting involved but I did, and did the best I could. I thought we were exploited by the Labour Party. Around that time they wound down the Young Socialists, and said that the Wedge would take the Young Socialists' place. But it shouldn't have been down to us. I felt we were manipulated. I've got a real mistrust for a lot of politicians, and I wouldn't get involved again. I should have stuck with my original instincts.

Billy (Bragg) is a very persuasive person, a very amiable, likeable person, and he's genuine, very into what he does. He was aware of what I distrusted, and he doesn't defend it either, but he sees the ultimate aim as much greater, and he's probably right. Before the Wedge, The Style Council had done a lot independently, raised a lot of money in benefits. But after the Wedge we were so disillusioned it all stopped. We were totally cynical about all of it. *1993*

They were a bunch of wankers (the Red Wedge). The Labour Party people as well. It wasn't me at all, I'm not into meetings and being part of somebody's club. I believed in what I believed in and a lot of those things I still do, but I'd never get involved again. We'd meet MPs around the country and they were more showbiz than the groups. It was an eye-opener, it brought me full circle in how I feel about politics. It's a game. I've very little interest in it. I'm not talking about what's happening to our planet or our country, but organised politics. Give me music any day of the week. *1995*

I still care. How can you not care? But in this last election, voting was a tokenistic thing. I was casting a vote against the Tories. I hate the way they're turning the recession on to people. It's our fucking fault now. Thatcher tells us we had too much credit, we bought too many houses. She encouraged us. On a brighter note… let's talk about my records. *1994*

If you're really from the working-class then you know how important clothes are to our culture. In the Sixties or Seventies any spare money went on clothes or records. That's the culture we created. But I noticed on the Red Wedge tour we'd get stick from the entourage for dressing in a certain way, with our loafers on or whatever. Were we supposed to walk around in dungarees? Boiler suits? It's nonsense, isn't it? That cloth-cap stuff is all bollocks. It's from before the time when pop culture started to happen. Mod was essentially a working-class movement. *1995*

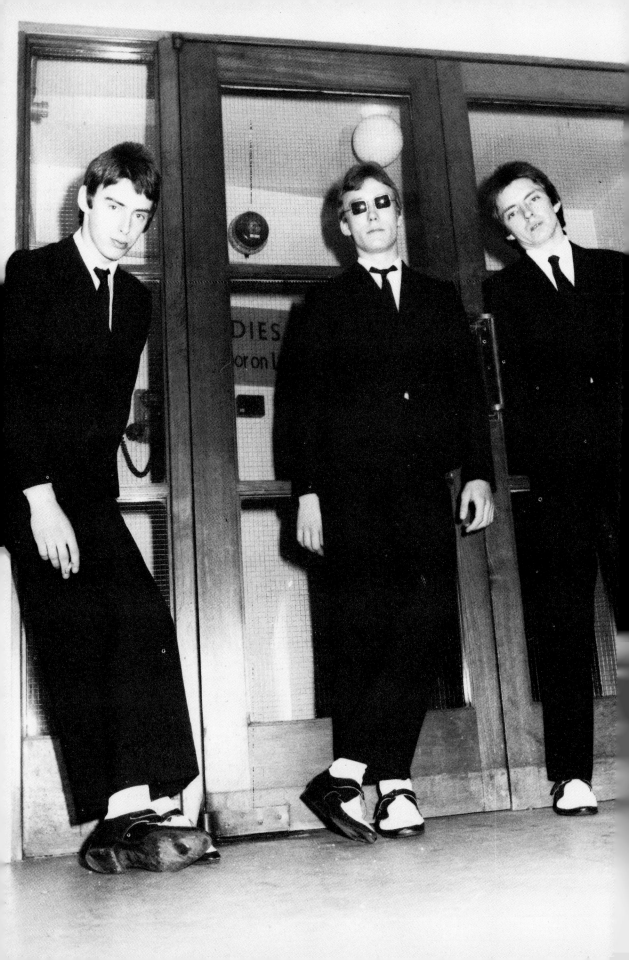

Keeping Counsel

Paul's Style

We'll probably change the clothes at sometime, but not drastically.
I still always wear that sort of thing (mohair suits). They're the sort of
clothes we like wearing. When we played the Nashville Rooms
recently a lot of kids turned out in black suits. It made it something
more than a gig, because they're all there for a real reason. I was
talking to one kid there who said that seeing us changed his way
of life. He was studying Arts and that, then he saw us and left school.
I'm not saying that's a good thing, but it's the sort of thing that's
happening.

 A lot of people are in it for dancing and having fun, which I
completely agree with, but a lot of people do get a message from it.
It's not a case of us shoving it down their throats, but we present
it and they take it or leave it. *1977*

I think style's important, more important than fashion. It's really
individualist, isn't it? Everyone's got their own perception of it. I want
to try and create this one image, one style, one direction. I like
mainstream fashions, you know, like you see the soul boys and girls
wearing. I think they wear fantastic clothes. I care what I look like,
which is down to personal dignity and pride, really. *1983*

If I have a style it's a combination of the Rickenbacker sound and
the fact that I play chords most of the time; I rarely play lead breaks.
Occasionally I've played finger style in the studio, but to be truthful
I have enough trouble with a flamin' pick! I'm not really a technical
type of player.

I chose a Rickenbacker originally just for the look, the sound
had little to do with it, but the fact that Pete Townshend played one
influenced me quite a lot, plus it was different. When I got used to
playing the guitar the sound of it began to appeal, but it wasn't my
first consideration. Now I have lots of Rickenbackers – I know it
sounds blasé, but I'm not even quite sure how many I have.

 The main instrument I use is a Rickenbacker 330 and I suppose
I must have about five of those. There's a pile of other guitars too, a
big Rickenbacker jazz model, a Gretsch Monkees Rock & Roll,
Rickenbacker 4001 bass, an Epiphone jazz guitar, Hofner Violin Bass,
a Rickenbacker 320, Rickenbacker 360 Stereo 12-string, Gibson SG,
and I'm trying to find one of the old Danelectro Long Horn Basses,
and a Paisley Fender Telecaster. We used a Telecaster on the
new single because it required that type of sound, but for live gigs
I've never been able to get the right sound out of that guitar for
all the songs.

Our sound man's always trying to get me to try new, different guitars because the Rickenbacker sound on stage is so uncontrollable, but I just go for the looks. *1981*

I'd say we're (Style Council) obsessed with clothes, yeah, but I don't think we ram that down people's throats other than wearing what we want to wear. I don't like being made to feel guilty for talking about clothes or being obsessed with clothes because it's decadent or it's not important. Who's to say? *1988*

Every Beatles record is different – you know, 'Abbey Road' is completely different from 'The White Album', which is completely different from 'Pepper'. I'm not comparing my work to theirs – it's in a different league – but it's the principle. I work at it, but I don't sit down and think, 'Maybe next year I'll do this and have that haircut'. Whatever I'm into at the time, I'm into, whether it changes or I'm completely at odds with it years later. At the time, I mean it. That's all that matters to me. *1995*

I've always been isolated. It's my own arrogance. *1995*

It's a bit Veronica Lake (Paul's least favourite haircut – the wedge) but it's also a bit kind of Perry Boy as well. I'd see some of the kids at Jam gigs in the early Eighties. It wasn't that dissimilar: long fringe here, short at that side. It was part sort of androgynous mod, and part casual. *1995*

My first scooter was a GP 150. I saved up for it and my Dad gave me some money. I was 17. Its original colour was turquoise but I got it sprayed black with yellow stripes down the side and I had my fly-screen with WOKING across it, and PAUL. And I had my mirrors in an X-shape, and a big rip aerial and my Mum had an old coat, not an Afghan but an old fur coat, and she cut it up and made it into some seat covers for me… I loved that scooter. *1995*

I've only got about five or six tops I wear. I haven't really got that many clothes, but everyone thinks I have. I mean, I love clothes, but I haven't really got that many. There's hardly anything I ever like in the shops, I'm so fussy. *1995*

I thought that was a fucking top idea (his moustache). I'm gonna grow the fucker back just to wind people up! *1996*

King Mod

I feel that the mod scene was very close to the punk thing; wholly youth – like going out with green hair. It changed you, made you something. It's something every kid goes through. You just want to be noticed. To be recognised.

I don't remember the original mods at all. I was much too young when all that happened. I suppose I was just attracted to the style of it all. *1979*

We're not trendsetters and it doesn't matter that it's a revival. Any movement's good that brings new ideas. The Purple Hearts' 'Millions Like Us' is just as relevant to our time as 'Anarchy' and 'In the City'. It's all about new kids being into new music. And it's definitely not us that started the fashion.

It (the current mod revival) just bores the arse off me. Just another movement like the skinheads and punks. The greatest irony that we could suffer would be a mods v punks thing. I mean there are already a load of mod bands like The Ricky Tics from Nottingham, The Purple Hearts from Barking, The Scooters from Coventry and I wish them all luck, but I'm not pledging my allegiance to any movement. I don't care who comes to see us.

If we started saying we were a mod band, it would be as bad as just another form of racialism. To me the mod dress is a private thing anyway. Rick and Bruce aren't into it really. If the mod revival did come back in a big way, we could easily become just a parody of ourselves. Like if it gets to the stage of beach fights and all that, then it's gone too far. *1979*

I still feel really steeped in the whole mod thing. I'll never ever lose that. I still think that whole look's brilliant, and to me The Small Faces were the perfect group... The Style Council's an extension of that.

I liked the way they kept it underground. That's not only the mod thing and the original skinheads and suedeheads, but also the original punk thing was like that. First time I saw The Pistols and The Clash I felt that same kind of thing: you walk down the 100 Club and nobody else outside that club knew what was going on down there in that little basement. *1984*

The Style Council records sound a lot better than fucking 'Wake Me Up Before You Go Go'. I think we won. Mods rule. *1995*

I always find it weird how things happen at a certain time. I mean, obviously The Jam were instrumental in part of it (the post-punk mod revival), but *Quadrophenia* came out round about then. That was still a big moment for a lot of kids, but the whole thing was pretty naf, wasn't it? Those groups were fucking awful. *1995*

It must have been weird to see me driving around on a scooter with a Parka on in 1975. *1995*

For me mod will never go out of fashion, and I think there will always be people who understand that and get what they want from it. I hate the way that it's getting used at the moment. I mean, I don't want to talk about bands individually, but they aren't mod bands are they? How can they be? It pisses me off a bit. It's like none of them are making mod records, no matter how mod they might look. If you want to hear a mod record stick on a good James Brown album. That's mod. *1996*

I've always kept the idea in my head about me still being a mod. It's like the album that never came out, the one Polydor refused to release – that was going to be called '1990: A New Decade In Modernism' because at the time I really believed that garage house was the new mod music. I remember, I'd go down the King's Road in '89 because I wanted to get some Kickers, and those other shoes, Wallabees, and I'd see all these kids queueing up in the shoe shops to get them. And just as they were standing there I saw a kid drive past on a pink scooter wearing a pastel coloured T-shirt, and I thought, this is mod, y'know... the kids buying all the imports! *1996*

Well, it's just a press thing isn't it, like all these fads? I mean, most of the groups took the look of mod and not the spirit. Anyway, mod will always be around in some shape or form because it's so classic. It's so ingrained in our culture and history. It'll always be there whether it's in high fashion or just in street fashion. *1995*

Union Jack

Weller vs. America

I do like England and I'm very conscious of the fact that I am English. But at the same time, 60 to 70 per cent of my influences are American, like R&B. And the English bands I like – The Small Faces, The Who – their influences are R&B as well. *1993*

There were two sides to the (Style Council's) French sleeve notes. One was being really pretentious trying to get other people's backs up, but on the other hand we were being quite serious. Everybody's looking at the big bad wolf that's supposed to be Russia, while through the back door the Americans are coming in. There's a lot more of that feeling in Europe than here.

  Britain's always been isolated in that way, in that culture, the things that appeal to us from America have been the trivial things really like deluxe fridges and all that shit, and the free-wheeling Cadillac kiddies. It's been no great cultural gain at all, totally the opposite. *1984*

We come from Britain and we're affected by British things.
What else can you do? Our environment reflects into what we write
and how we sound, so there's no way you can change it. It's just a
compromise to do anything other than that. That's why we'll never be
successful outside of Britain, I don't think. I mean, you listen to
any British records that make it in the States, for instance, that are
supposedly by new bands. It's always like Joe Jackson and
The Police. It's all American-sounding, or if not American sort of
universal-sounding.

The one Clash single that made it into the American charts
was 'Train In Vain' which was like the fucking Doobie Brothers or Nils
Lofgren or something. But I can understand it. I mean, to some Yank
or something listening to 'That's Entertainment', it probably sounds
like a load of gobbledegook. *1981*

I think (The Jam) sold about 150,000 copies of 'Sound Affects',
which is a drop in the ocean over there. It's not a defeatist way of
looking at it, it's just, what else can you do? It's our sound and
we ain't gonna change it and that's it. It doesn't really stop us playing
anywhere. Every place we've played we've always gone down
really well and communicated anyway, despite language barriers.
So it's only the records that don't sell, and in the States a lot of that's
only due to radio.

People won't pick up on us cos it doesn't sound right.
Our records are rated, er, what's the phrase… AOR. Is that right?
'Adult Oriented Radio' – it's sorta like late-night crap. Music over
there's really conservative. People talk about conservative England,
but America's far worse. *1981*

We (The Jam)'d like to be successful in America because we
don't know where else to take it now. But if you look at the American
charts, Samantha Fox is at Number 10. It makes you think, why
the fuck are we bothering really. But you have to soldier on. America
will accept any old shit these days. At the moment we're probably
selling about 70 to 100,000 copies of each LP in America which
sounds a lot but it's a piss in the ocean compared to the size of the
country. If the record company says they're going to break an act,
then they break – it's kind of like a foregone conclusion that it's going
to happen. It's all bent over there, but they've never decided to
break us in the States. It's fucking really weird. You just think why the
fucking hell do we bother? *1988*

I'm not being nationalistic, but it's great when you can feel
proud about English pop music again. Most of those American bands
just sound the same to me. Which ones? I've no idea, I get their
names mixed up. You know, like that lot who cut their pants off at
the bottom. I don't buy all that nihilism stuff. Life can't be that crap,
especially not if you're in a group. There has to be a few joyful
moments. It's a pretty good job. *1995*

The Bitterest Pill

Fame & Publicity

I don't want to make rash statements. I tend to hold back...
I wouldn't say I was dishonest, though. It's just I don't want to say
something that two hours later I will completely disagree with.
I haven't got the answers, any answers, and I never like to pretend
that I have. I have to be cautious.

I like the colours (of the Union Jack). Everyone brings it up – just
shows the power of the press, dunnit? It was good, though, it made
us a lot of enemies, which we wanted to. *1978*

This is gonna sound like a massive cliché, but everything I've got
to say comes out in the records. Just because I ain't got so much to
go on about in interviews, which'll make boring reading, it don't
follow that I'm a dull and simple lad. *1978*

I don't know how success affects me, it's hard to say. I don't think
it affects me in an egotistical way. Whenever I say that, people think
I'm being complacent about things, taking too much in my stride,
but I'm not. Actually, I find fame unnerving, embarrassing. *1981*

I used to be really cocky in interviews. Now I just get more and more
nervous every time I do one. *1981*

The Press slagged off Adam and the Ants for years, they were
really despised but they've come through. They wrote us off a few
years ago, but the thing is if you've got a strong enough following
you can come through it anyway. *1981*

I like seeing my photo in papers and I liked being on the telly! A lot
of people moan about it but I don't really believe them when they say
they don't like it. I cut out photos and keep them in files. I've got
special Style Council files and I keep the cuttings in them. I file them
record by record because most of our press is when a record comes
out – I keep ad, posters, everything. *1984*

I get loads of fan mail and tapes sent to the office. I have a big
box of letters there. I try and take a few letters home every night and
answer them. Sometimes I actually manage to do it but a lot of times
they just collect up at home so I've got two boxes of them, one at the
office and one at home. *1984*

I was very, very disillusioned with things (the 1987 downturn in
Weller's popularity), so the last thing on my mind was whether I was
in touch with being popular or not. I just lost interest in music for a
while, lost sight of what I should be doing. The last serious thing

I did was 'Confessions Of A Pop Group', which most people fucking hated but I thought was really good. I thought there was some very clever stuff on 'Confessions', but the fact that people didn't really like it made me doubt all that. When you believe in something and people turn around and say 'I can't hear it', it kind of throws you. *1993*

In interviews it's always one thing or the other – the 'serious' interview where we talk politics or just total trivia. But there's got to be room for both. I like sort of talking about socks. *1985*

I never was a spokesman for youth or whatever they decided to say about me. But that's all stopped now, ain't it? I never took that seriously or anything. It's just another media cliché, really. I thought Morrissey was the spokesman now. I thought he'd rather taken that mantle over from me, if I ever had it. Or Bono. I thought he was another one, isn't he? I'm out of touch with it all… All that 'spokesman' stuff was because of stuff we done like Red Wedge and the media only saw us as Billy Bragg going on tour or having a photograph with Neil Kinnock or something and it wasn't just about voting good old Neil in. It extends a lot further than that, but the media just concentrate on the pop-star bullshit. *1988*

Maybe it's my complexes, but I get the impression that most people dislike me anyway, so I always start every conversation from that point. It can only get better. People have so many preconceptions about me. *1993*

Almost every time I read an article about me I don't recognise the person that they're talking about. Not in any respect. But of course everyone has an image of themselves which is very different to how other people perceive them. What's the most popular misconception about me? That I'm miserable, I suppose. I don't really care. What's the opposite? That I'm always laughing and having fun. I'm just like anyone – I'm neither all of the time. I'm serious when I get on stage and I'm serious about my music, but I definitely like a good time.
   I guess I was pretty uptight in The Jam, but I'm a lot more grown-up about things now. I certainly consider myself approachable; I'm forever being stopped in the street for a chat. I know a lot of people have already made up their minds about me, though. But I'm not here to change their opinion – that's their problem, not mine. *1995*

I can't stand *Q* (the magazine), it's a load of intellectual bollocks. That's not what music should be about. *1995*

Half the time people just write about me – having a personal dig, very rarely arguing on a musical basis. I can't get too upset about it, 'cos it's never been any different, but sometimes it gets too much and I have to have a word. There's only a few times I've ever felt insulted: mainly because it's been something personal, or someone writing about me and Dee. It's like, what the fuck has this got to do with

anyone? I don't like it when it's insulting to me and my family.
Like me and Dee splitting up getting in the tabloids. I'm not used to it.
Dee went on Breakfast TV the other day to plug her record and the
first thing they asked is about me and her splitting up. They wouldn't
ask me that. *1995*

Image, Videos & Visuals

I don't watch *Top Of The Pops* very often to be honest, and I don't
really care about it one way or the other. People get too excited about
it. The charts have always been there and most of the stuff in the
charts is crap anyway. From any era a lot of the good records never
make the Top 10, never make Number 1, and it's the same thing
today. *1984*

I hate the way videos take precedence over the music,
especially in America. I don't think any group's made a great film,
with the exception of maybe *A Hard Day's Night*. It's always been
rags to riches, all that cliché shite. I'd like not to be cast as
musicians, it's just a question of finding the right kind of story.
Joe Orton wrote a screenplay for The Beatles which they never used,
and I thought the idea of Orton teaming up with The Beatles was
brilliant. Someone else told me about Andrew Loog Oldham trying to
buy *A Clockwork Orange* for the Stones in the Sixties. It was that kind
of idea we were looking for. That pairing up. *1984*

All the concepts I had in The Council were crazy, nonsense. I had more ideas and concepts than music. I think people misunderstood our sense of humour, though, Do you remember 'JerUSAlem'? I hate videos, but so many of ours were piss-takes of videos and of ourselves. People never got the jokes. In 'Long Hot Summer', me and Mick Talbot were rubbing each other's earlobes – the homo-erotic bit – and after it was finished, I got a call from the MD. He says: 'This is no good. There's no women in this video. What's going on here?' So, in the next one we did, for 'Solid Bond', we put in lots of fast-cut clips from porno movies, people shagging each other. And I called him up and said: 'There you are. This one's got lots of women in it. Plenty of birds for you'. *1994*

We were trying too hard. I was trying to get away from the stereotype of this miserable moaner. We went too much the other way. You know, we thought the videos were really funny: they made us and a few of our friends laugh, because we all got the joke – but that isn't good enough. There's a thin line between doing what you want to do and indulgence. I guess we crossed that barrier. *1995*

I enjoy doing photo sessions now – with The Jam we'd play up with the photographers a bit which was stupid and childish but we'd done it so much we were a bit blasé. Now I really try and work with the photographers to try to get the best out of everything and also try and come up with some ideas. We try to get a lot of detail into our sleeves and adverts and everything and I want it to be the same with photographs. Me and Mick will find out what each other is going to wear – not to match them up but just so we have an idea. *1984*

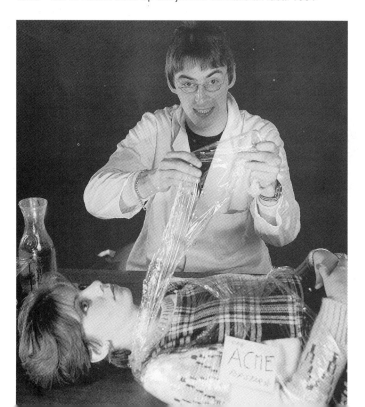

Right: With Respond singer, Tracie Young.

Above: Supergrass.
Below: Liam and Noel Gallagher.

It's like that cat in Wet Wet Wet who's always smiling. I don't know what he finds so funny. Why should we be grinning all the time? Why should we play the game? It's a fucking stupid game if you have to be jolly. Funny old world, innit?

I don't think my records are part of the Blur and Oasis thing, I don't think my success this year has been related to that at all. No-one's gonna buy my record just because Noel said it's good. Another generation have just come along and not bothered with Sonic The Hedgehog, that's all. Look at this year, Black Grape, The Charlatans, Blur, Supergrass, all big British pop albums. And suddenly Bon Jovi and AC/DC aren't going to Number 1 any more. Things have just come full circle. *1995*

I probably know more musicians now than ever before. And not because I hang out in trendy bars or the Groucho or something; I've just got respect for more players now. And most of the time, they're probably 10 years younger than me. We just seem to have more in common: Oasis, The Charlatans, Primals, Blur. I'm not talking about me hanging around with my famous friends, just the fact that we're doing it for the same reasons.

I like Noel (Gallagher, Oasis)'s songs. It's an obvious thing, but he's a fucking good writer, and whether the knives are drawn for him now or not doesn't matter, because he's got it. He'll just get better and better. There are some great songs on the new LP – 'Don't Look Back In Anger' is a classic. *1995*

Oasis seem to appreciate all the good values of being in a pop group. They know that when it's done properly, music still means something to people. I like Supergrass, too. I've been playing their LP a lot. They've got the plot: they can play their instruments and they know what a proper song is – good melody and good structure. I like almost anyone who can go out and do it, and mean it. That's the sort of group I was brought up on. *1995*

How long do you reckon before the backlash? Another year, maybe? Nah, I don't give a fuck about it any more. I just find it really funny. Everything goes in cycles. the only thing I don't like about it is that it makes me very cynical. It's not healthy. *1995*

What does George Michael expect? Live by the tabloids, die by the tabloids. *1995*

I didn't go to Earl's Court, but Oasis getting so big is great. It's a real buzz – and for all those people who said that computer games or comedy or any of that crap were the new rock'n'roll a few years ago – it's proved they were all fucking wrong. Rock'n'roll dies out for a while, then it always comes back. *1996*

Big Boss Groove

Songwriting

Of course I was like The Clash – the bands that made me think
I should be writing about something a little more important. I mean,
I did get that much from them so in a way they did start something.
But I still write what I consider relevant lyrics anyway like 'Non-stop
Dancing'. I used to know this geezer who was really into Northern
Soul, and a very important part of his life was dancing, which I
thought was really great. *1977*

There's more involvement as a group now, but if I write a song, I've
got my own set ideas about it. It's the same with Bruce. But we've
always worked as a group anyway. *1977*

I'd be too embarrassed to write something like 'we're all going
down the pub' even though that is probably real to thousands of kids,
and very truthful. I just feel that I should reach for something higher.
I think music is an art form. A highly abused art form. *1978*

The words are really important in my songs. I think it's sad that
words have become a bit unfashionable – no-one's that bothered
about lyrics. A lot of records which I really like – dance records –
which have got good grooves in them and are great to dance to, the
words always let them down. They're often not even good pop lyrics,
or good love songs, usually they're just inane. Kool and The Gang
are brilliant, I think you should try and use all the song. Every bit of it.
Motown did it. They kept the groove but they still had good lyrics.
In the Seventies people like The Temptations and Curtis Mayfield
managed to do it with political lyrics.
   An idea for a song with me usually starts with the title. I think
over the years my songwriting has become more direct. I don't use
characters any more, I don't use situations any more, I usually just
write what I feel. Some of the things I've written recently I think are
a little bit filmic, stuff like 'Paris Match', where I can imagine pictures
in my head.

I like Ben Watt and Tracey Thorn (Everything But The Girl).
Those two together I think are a really good combination. They write
really good lyrics and a lot of their stuff is melodically quite clever,
well structured. I like Animal Nightlife, I think they're really underrated.
Andy Polaris, the singer, writes the words, I think, and they start off
with an interesting title and a good idea which hooks people and
makes you want to find out what the song's about. They take
everyday things and add something else to them. I used to like The
Beatles a lot but now I think they're really overrated when you look
at some of their songs. But melodically they were always good and
the structures of their songs were always good.

I suppose in some ways I write in an old-fashioned way because I always have middle-eights in my songs and not many people do any more. It's usually just a verse and chorus. Structure is really important. Some I've really had to work at, others come really quickly. Keeping the whole thing interesting, that's what it all comes down to. *1984*

When we finished 'Setting Sons', I got the engineer to play the whole album backwards for me to listen to on cassette, and there was just that one little piece of music, of backward vocal that I really liked the melody of. So I wrote the whole of 'Dreams Of Children' built around that, more-or-less made up on the spot. As to the psychedelic feel, we'd done this American tour and me and Bruce just listened to The Beatles' 'Revolver' all the time. It's still my favourite Beatles album.

'The Dreams Of Children' was recorded after 'Going Underground' but we felt it was such a strong track that we didn't want it to be lost on a B-side. But double A-sides don't work – one track always gets played more than the other and will get promoted more. *1992*

The lyrics and feel on 'Tales From The Riverbank' are completely different. And 'Riverbank' has a different mood, a mystic feel. I still really like it – it makes me think of Woking and my childhood – and it should have been the A-side. I hate 'Absolute Beginners' now – it was a fill-in track for me, a stop-gap. I was creatively exhausted by that time. 'Sound Affects' was a hard album to finish because I didn't have many songs upfront. 1981 provided a year off to get the stuff together for the next LP, 'The Gift' – because 1982 was another prolific year. *1992*

I published some of my own poetry (in the early Eighties Paul helped to run the Riot Stories publishing house). Most of it was complete bollocks, but I did a reading at the Poetry Olympics Michael Horowitz organised in 1982. That was fucking hard, although I thought I did all right at the time. The poems weren't exactly Wilfred Owen. I've tried to forget about it, but I can remember the black mohair suit I was wearing, and my desert boots. *1994*

My favourite Style Council songs? Most of the lyrics on 'Our Favourite Shop' and most of 'Confessions'. I was talking about the title track of 'Confessions' the other night: all these really slick images come at you really quickly, kind of parodying all the sort of 1980s marketing nonsense at that time. They're very good lines. We should have left it there. It would have been a good swan song. *1995*

I'm not 17 any more. I'm just not interested in what I was writing about in The Jam. It's a natural progression for me. Some people haven't got a clue, though. I read one review that described 'Woodcutter's Son' as pastoral. That's shit. Nothing about that song is fuckin' pastoral. Then there was that guy from Gene.

The guitarist, what's he called? Looks like a bit of a clone. He said:
'Oh, Weller's entering his Humble Pie phase.' Like I'm so fuckin'
calculated. Just because he's in a band that base their every move
on someone else. I'll smack him if I ever meet him. No, hang on.
I won't. I'm into peace and love now. *1995*

I'm wary of songs that are autobiographical. They might start off
being about me but after that I'm a professional songwriter, just trying
to come up with something that will intrigue people. But parts of
'Porcelain God' are about me… not because I see myself as any kind
of God, but I am disappointed in myself. It's about me talking to my
missus, then the rest of the song is about something else. *1995*

Everyone works better under pressure, it's like when there's a war on,
everyone stands together. I'm prolific in three week bursts then I have
long dry periods. *1978*

My songwriting's become more personalised, but I wouldn't
really call it introverted. I'm writing maybe more from… I was gonna
say from a personal angle, but I think I always have done anyway.
Maybe it sorta shows more now. *1981*

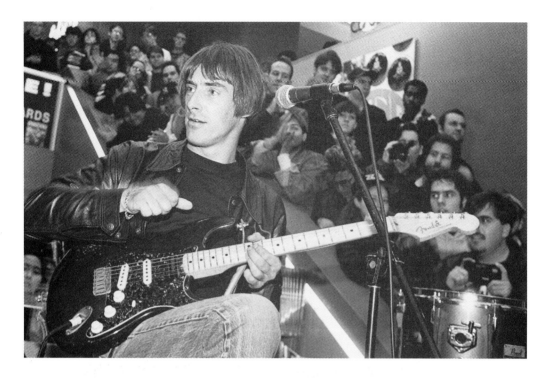

I wrote differently at different times (during The Jam days). The songs that are always easier to record are the ones that are very complete – where you play them to the band or producer and you know exactly what the song is because it's all there for you. You hear the verse, you hear the bridge and the chorus and then we have a little musical link. But that wasn't the way with all the tracks and some of them, especially the later stuff after 'Setting Sons' – and 'Sound Affects' in particular – were scraps of ideas and images. *1992*

'Eton Rifles' was based on a Right To Work march in '79. They all marched past Eton and they were getting a right ticking-off from the chaps inside. I just thought it was quite amusing – 'Eton Rifles' with all those army cadets. They all go and play war games up in the fields. Again, it was quite easy to write because I had all the images in front of me, so all I had to do was get a handle on the thing. *1992*

I really like 'Into Tomorrow', and I think 'Porcelain Gods' is one of the best lyrics I've ever written. I just think it's really powerful. The lines could mean a million different things to people… A lot of people I knew thought it was about gear, but I meant it to be about success. It's all over the shop: fractured, but it all makes sense to me. They're all really powerful images… good poetry. *1995*

'That's Entertainment' is really good, although it was a bit of a steal. The idea came from this poem in a fanzine, and I wrote it when I was drunk! Just shows you, there's no pattern to it. A lot of the stuff on 'Sound Affects': 'Monday's great, 'Man In The Corner Shop's good. 'Town Called Malice'. My voice is good on that, too. *1995*

Taking Ecstasy didn't make me go home and write five songs in a certain way because I'd dropped one. *1995*

I like the lyrics on 'Stanley Road'… they're as good as, or maybe the best ones I've ever done. I'll try and go more with what sounds really good now, hopefully without being banal. It's okay to write a great line, but if you don't sing it right, or it doesn't sound right, or it doesn't flow, then you miss it anyway. That's what I tend to concentrate on now: the instinctive side. *1995*

The Small Faces, Sixties stuff I hadn't listened to for years, put me back in touch with what I'd forgotten I was good at, which is playing guitar. *1995*

The early songs were just straight Beatle rip-offs. We'd get that songbook, 'The Beatles Complete', and go through the chords… So nothing's changed, really. I was into Merseybeat as well, Gerry and The Pacemakers. For me it's always been Sixties music. I guess the first things you hear are always the most influential. *1995*

My Ever Changing Views

Paul On Others

I still think a load of the Sixties bands were a lot more creative than most around now. I think that's what we're trying to work to – something that's in some way innovative. *1977*

I think The Nips, Shane McGowan's band, are really promising. He's one of the original punks – he's got to be someone some day. I like Patrik Fitzgerald, who did the tour with us and there's a group called The Passengers... there's a lot of little groups. The trouble is that none of the record companies are putting any money into them anymore. In 1977 they were going crazy. Now suddenly, they're all shitting out cause there's no more money in it. The best things to come out of the new wave are happening now anyway. *1979*

Townshend has been putting something back with his Eel Pie Records, so I think that geezer's alright. I really do. Now if I'm going to slag anyone off it should be people like me and Joe Strummer. I'm bursting with fucking ideas to do something like that but it all takes money. When I said those things about Townshend, I was pretty naïve. It all takes money. It's a vicious circle. I can't do nothing until I've got the money.
   I'd love to have a publishing company so that I could publish young poets, people like Dave Waller. No-one gives a crap about people like him. All they want to read is Shelley and Keats and people like that. I'd love to have a record company to help young bands. But it all takes bread, and right now I haven't got that sort of bread. But if I don't do that when I have got the bread, then I'm the biggest cunt out... and all the other bands as well. *1979*

I don't like the crappy slogans Wham! have got – 'Make It Big' and 'Go For It'. Go for fucking what? An all year suntan? *1985*

Wham! early 80's.

I thought the best thing about The Small Faces was the fact that they were all the same height and kind of looked quite similar... I suppose we're similar heights... but I think my other favourite group is The Modern Jazz Quartet because they really come across as being a group and inside the group they all have kind of little separate roles, like one takes care of the business and one looks after the transport, know what I mean? That's a proper group. It works as a unit because they all have their separate roles. I really like to see that in a group. *1988*

The first thing I heard by The Small Faces was 'Tin Soldier' in maybe late 1967. This is just a great album. It's very underrated

The Small Faces, c.1967.

and not really recognised... people seem to forget about this one. This was the first time they were left alone in the studio and given as much time as they wanted. There's some really good songs there. Funnily enough, it's never been reissued in its entirety – they've always missed tracks off it, or put it out in a different sleeve.

There was that 'Darlings Of Wapping Wharf Launderette' with two or three tracks missing there. If you don't reissue a record properly then why bother? Make it a compilation. I was still too young to be aware of where they were at image-wise, but I remember liking the way they looked. *1992*

I was only familiar with the Traffic singles when I was a kid – 'Paper Sun' and 'Mulberry Bush', 'Hole In My Shoe'. I was a pop kid then and I was really into all that stuff. This record's ('Traffic') got some great playing on it – you know 'Feelin' Alright'? The Dave Mason track? Brilliant. The playing and the feel generally is really classic. Those acoustic sounds... it's sort of given me a different scope as well – made me think differently about music and what I can do with it. And it's got lovely packaging. *1992*

I like Marvin Gaye's Sixties stuff, but not as much as the album 'What's Going On', when he started getting serious. It runs like a suite – it's almost like a classical movement, the tracks all running into each other. It's got an overall sound... the fact that he's using the same chords on different tracks and stuff. Have you ever seen that film Expo '72? He does a couple of tracks from this album – it was obviously from around the same time – and he runs three or four of the tracks into each other. It's like a classical or jazz movement the way he does it. *1992*

Curtis Mayfield was really on the case – right up until his accident he was still making good records. He's not that fashionable and he didn't follow trends, he just had his own sound. It's his lyrics and his whole attitude and comment on what was happening at that time which make him good. It may be a bit different now, but in the early Seventies he really had his finger on the pulse, like Gil Scott-Heron. It's so humanist as well... I've met him a couple of times and you can tell he's genuine. He likes people, and that comes out in his music. He's kind of like a Buddah figure. *1992*

The Clash made me think about lyrics. I feel like I've always tried to write good words, but to hear things like 'Career Opportunities' – that was the sort of stuff that would never get into songs. It was really contemporary as well. *1992*

Very few people deserve the title 'genius', but I think Stevie Wonder's a real musical genius. Not because of the fact he's blind – that's by-the-by really – but because he can play almost every

Above: Morrissey.
Below: Duran Duran.

instrument apart from the guitar and bass really well, and he's also a great drummer. He's a brilliant songwriter – he's got a great sense of melody. Some of his lyrics are really good, though they're not his strongest point, but musically he's so clever with his chords, he uses a lot of jazz chords but within a different structure... brilliant. *1992*

Morrissey? He's too English and too white and too melancholy. I've got a bit of that, I guess, but not as much as him. Not my thing at all, but some people like to revel in it. I can't see the point. I'm not a particularly outgoing person, though I have my moments, but I like outgoing, positive people. I like some aspects of America because of that. *1993*

I used to worry about not being intellectual enough, but now I see things for what they are. I'm not good at that and it doesn't interest me. I don't understand what Bono – or Bownow, or however you pronounce it – is trying to tell me. Is it that the world is shit and false? Well, I knew that already. Why is he always swaggering? Why that mock rock-star arrogance? What's the concept? Why not just be a rock star and get on with it. I like 'Rattle And Hum'. I understood the attack on the IRA and the Martin Luther King bit. But I don't get him now. *1994*

What did I think of Robbie leaving Take That? Well, not much. They're just a pop band. If the kid had a fantastic voice it'd be different. But it's hardly Paul leaves The Beatles, is it? *1995*

I know this will sound sacrilegious to their long-term fans but I only got into Van Morrison and Neil Young in the last three years. So I've got no prejudices; I don't think 'Astral Weeks' is necessarily Van's best album; the first thing I heard of Neil Young's was 'Harvest Moon', just the simplicity of it is fucking great. Same with Van, some of the tracks on 'Hymns To The Silence' are at least as good as 'Moondance'. I just like whatever is good, now. Same with my own music now: I wouldn't not do a tune because it sounds too country or too rock. As long as it feels right and natural, that's the criterion. *1995*

Bollocks. Fucking bollocks. I've still got edge in my music, hopefully always will have – and if my music ever got as laid-back and mellow as Eric Clapton's I'd pack it in. Or shoot myself. (On being christened 'the Eric Clapton of the 1990s.) *1995*

You can't blame me for the New Romantics... I'm an old romantic. Terrible, wasn't it? There seemed to be a lot of the old punks involved. They went underground for a while and resurfaced in frills. I've never lived in North London, you see. That's quite important. *1995*

With Macca and Noel.

I thought Duran Duran, Spandau Ballet, Depeche Mode, Living In A Box (who shared a plane trip home from Italy with Style Council) were a bunch of wankers, all walking around like peacocks, when, musically, none of them were any fucking good. None of them could sing or play or write a decent fucking tune. You know, do that and then walk around with your chest out. That applies to The Council as well, I suppose, after a certain point.

When you compare yourself to people like Winwood, like McCartney – that's what you should be striving for. Not the flashy clothes. If they come first and the music comes second... that's why the Eighties were so shit. *1995*

Whenever I see Noel (Gallagher -- Oasis) he's quite together. I've only seen him frothing at the mouth once. *1995*

'Redemption Song' by Bob Marley is pretty good to me. There's nothing clever about that – and it's more powerful than anything Morrissey ever fucking wrote. *1995*

I saw The Smiths in Newcastle, on the Red Wedge tour, and the intensity and the power... as soon as they hit the boards it was obvious. I suppose that I hadn't seen that since The Jam days: that kind of passion and fury. I still couldn't hear it in the records though – I liked some of them, but they were never that explosive.

Morrissey himself doesn't do anything for me at all. Some of the words are all right, but I'm not really into literary lyrics. I like things to be really simple. That's why I like R&B songs. I just don't like things to be that wordy. *1995*

I used to love Wilko Johnson (of R&B band Feelgood), he was like the English Chuck Berry. I went to see them in the Guildford Civic. He came out, did this huge lick with his legs out and they were off. Yeah! It's like that Lennon quote when he went to see a rock'n'roll movie and he thought, now that's a good job, I'd like to do that. *1995*

That thing in *Mojo* really annoyed me. 'Five Bands Who've Reinvented Themselves', which apparently was supposed to be just a humorous piece. But to put me among Duran Duran and George Michael, that I take as a personal insult. It ain't funny. It's probably the most insulted I've felt for a long time. How can you compare me to Duran Duran? It's nonsense. *1995*

The Clash became just like any other rock band. All those pictures of them in biker jackets with their hands in their pockets, like 'we might be holding a gun'. Or a fucking water pistol. And the Pistols records just got worse and worse; all that multi-layered guitar. Years later, they sound like real mainstream rock, don't they? It's only the vocals that make it sound like something else. *1995*

I don't feel part of some big music club. Just because we all play guitars, we're supposed to get on. It doesn't work that way, obviously, although I would go up and talk to someone backstage if I liked them. We had our photos taken with Bo Diddley yesterday. He signed some stuff for us as well, which was wicked. It's fantastic to meet someone like that, someone I respect. We dedicated 'Woodcutter's Son' to him, because it uses that guitar sound that he originated. He came up to us later and told us it was great. He's 66, but he looks really fit. He was handing out these cards to the kids with his photo and 'Just Say No To Drugs' on them. I had to hide a spliff behind my back. *1995*

Above: The Clash.
Below: Culture Club.

Sheryl Crow's got a nice voice, but I didn't like her songs. *1996*

I liked 'Time' (Culture Club). That was a great record. And 'Do You Really Want To Hurt Me' was good. Boy George sounded all right at first. But it's funny, when I hear a lot of those Eighties singers, they don't seem to have moved on. They sound weedy to me now. *1995*

I'd never watch a band like R.E.M. I don't like stupid, wimpy music. I like music with bollocks to it – which doesn't necessarily entail guitars turned up and played full throttle, either. Just meat and potatoes, know what I mean? R.E.M. are all very nice chaps, though. *1995*

The Pistols and The Clash were the two groups for me, the first contemporary groups that I'd ever liked. There are groups I've gone back to from the early Seventies and checked out, like Free, and I really like them now but not at the time. When punk came, at last there were some groups more or less the same age. And the details – they had short hair straight trousers, they didn't have beards. It made a difference to me, because I was a mod by this time, and they used to play covers like 'Substitute', and Troggs tracks. *1995*

Uh Huh Oh Yeh

Other Angles On Weller

Above: A young Pete Townshend.
Below: Boy George, post-Culture Club.

I have never come across any other artist or writer who is so afraid of appearing hypocritical. But he is a Star. He himself carefully engineers what kind of Star and in what kind of atmosphere he shines: never too grand, never too remote. *Pete Townshend, 1982*

Weller's strength is that he uses imagery deep in the English psyche. *Billy Bragg*

He is to Little England what Helena Bonham-Carter is to Edwardiana. *Melody Maker, 1994*

There's few songwriters that inspire me. People like Lennon and Weller. *Liam Gallagher, 1995*

Whenever he came he was very nervous. Clearly he wanted to come, do the work and then leave as soon as possible. He was quite short with me. But when it was finished he rang and said, 'Sorry, I was so shy I couldn't talk to you. I'm really pleased with it and I'm really happy you could do it'. *Artist Peter Blake talking about his client and the sleeve for 'Stanley Road', 1996*

I remember that I found him very cold. Perhaps because I was expecting Diana Ross and I got Gilbert O'Sullivan. *Boy George, 1984*

He looked a bit of a prat really, but at least they looked up from their pints. *Rick Buckler on Paul wearing nothing but a collar, cuffs and tie at a Jam gig, 1993*

Paul Weller? He's like the kid at school who was in remedial class, and he'd 'ave spit between his two top teeth, and then flick his cigarette over the school fence as a sign of rebellion. It's all very well maturin' at 26, but when yer just maturin' into a fifth-form remedial, what's the point?' *Echo and the Bunnymen's Ian McCulloch, 1984*

He is a small businessman, and when he goes to negotiate his deal, and talks to his banker, he thinks in a Conservative, free-enterprise mentality – yet when he writes his lyrics, his experience simply isn't used. He talks about the class struggle, and perpetrates the myth that people are different. It's a derisive, destructive thing, and that the pop world helps to encourage it is just an appalling situation. *Police manager Miles Copeland, 1985*

He was a meal ticket for those boys (The Jam), but they fell out in a big way. *John Weller, Paul's father and manager, 1994*

Paul came to me and said 'I'm gonna split the group' and I said: 'No, you wait until you finish the album, because there are debts to be met and wages to be paid.' *John Weller, 1994*

The biggest mistake Polydor made with Paul was rejecting the solo album he made at the end of The Council. Doesn't matter what they thought of it. If you know anything about artists, you'll realise they should have let him get that out of his system. He'll never forget that. *John Weller, 1994*

I first met Paul when I was in a band called The Boys. I went down to his studio to give him a demo. I think I saw him once after that – and the next thing was playing on 'The Weaver'. Was it a shock? Oh yeah. He means a lot to people our age, doesn't he? He first got me into playing music.

   After 'Wild Wood', he said 'I'm gonna make an album better than this', and I was thinking 'yeah, right'. And then I heard this album ('Stanley Road') coming together. And it is; it's his best album to date. I'd put it next to 'Abbey Road' or something, but I know Paul'd just say 'it's just a good record'. That's what he's like. *Steve Cradock, guitarist and right-hand man, 1996*

I always liked The Style Council more than The Jam, but I think what Paul's doing now is by far the best he's done. It just sounds different to what he's done before. He's come of age, I think, and it really shows. *Soul singer and 'Stanley Road' sessioneer Carleen Anderson, 1996*

When Paul got rid of us to go solo we were at our biggest. It left Rick and me in the lurch a bit and we haven't seen him since. I don't hate Paul and I suppose I'd buy him a pint if I bumped into him – but that's about it. *Jam bassist Bruce Foxton, 1991*

Paul was such a prolific songwriter, too. He never stopped delivering great material. As soon as we'd got an album finished he'd be writing new songs for the next single. You forget that things like 'Funeral Pyre', 'Absolute Beginners', 'Beat Surrender', 'When You're Young' and 'Strange Town' were never put on any albums. I think we released 16 singles in five years: they weren't all great, but there certainly wasn't a duff one, which is a pretty major achievement in my book. *Dennis Munday of Polydor, The Jam's record company, 1992*

Things like 'Pretty Green' grew out of Paul picking up on a rhythmic idea that Bruce and I were messing about with one day. Or else we'd experiment with some of Bruce's bass lines, to link sections for two different songs which weren't quite working and turn them into one that did. That sort of thing. You may think this is sour grapes, but my feeling is that Paul needed Bruce and I to be there to bounce ideas off. He fed off the tension. Once he took sole control of things, I think a lot of the fire went out. *The Jam's Rick Buckler, 1992*

It was a real shock when it happened. We knew Paul wasn't happy, and I was expecting him to suggest taking a break for six months or a year so he could concentrate on getting his studio and record label together. Then he'd come back refreshed, and we'd pick it all up again. After all, right from the start, when I first joined the band from school in 1973, the idea was always to be big. And despite the fact that we were massive in Britain, the US was only just beginning to open up for us, and we still had a lot of work to do.

The trouble was that Paul never discussed what he was feeling with us. And he hasn't done since. I've only met him once since we split up, although I've tried to contact him several times, which makes me sad. Maybe he was right: maybe we couldn't have persevered with the new direction he was moving in. But I always thought Rick and myself were amiable enough chaps to give it a go if he'd asked us. But he never did. *Bruce Foxton, 1992*

Paul Weller's a good old git. People think he's some deep god, but he's a moany old bastard. He's like Victor Meldrew with a suntan. He's a nice bloke, I love him like the day is long and he's so honest. Too honest maybe.

He was aware that these bands were coming up and embracing The Jam but he'd never met any of them. So he was quite curious as to what anybody actually thought of him. What struck me was how aware he was of the music scene. I thought he'd be sat wherever he lives and not heard about Blur and Supergrass or whoever, but he talked to me about Dodgy, The Boo Radleys and The Primals, he knew every single band and the records and what he thought about them.

The weird thing is that because we've got so many young fans, they were coming up to me asking who that old bloke playing with us on piano was! We're going, 'That, right that's fucking Paul Weller!' They're going 'What does he do?' Then you realise these kids are 11, 12 and they've never heard The Jam.
Oasis's Noel Gallagher, 1995

Below: Oasis, 1996.

Into Tomorrow

The Future

It's getting harder and harder to sell original ideas to people, these days. Everybody wants something safe and something that they know. It's like they want to go out and buy Sade's new LP or Sting's because they know what they're going to get. So it's frustrating for us. I'd like to have the recognition we deserve. It would be nice to get that without all the mega-star crap.

  I feel sorry for the creative people in this country because one of the national characteristics of this country is a suspicion of anything new and different. I think it'll be the destruction of pop music in the end. Even of art. I don't know. *1988*

Perhaps some of my stuff will stand up in time, although not necessarily in terms of the performances or production. The sort of thing that seems to hold up is always the non-political stuff, songs with universal messages. Love songs. *1992*

Yes, music's a vocation. How long can I do this? I'd like to think I'll be doing it until I drop, but does it have to become diluted? I don't want to end up making bland cabaret showbiz bollocks. 'Remember this one, folks?' That's why we disliked Max Bygraves and Val Doonican, because we had The Beatles and the Stones. Now I can look at Neil Young and Van Morrison, who are still valid and prolific. Well, that's two people. Do we have a certain time and then it finishes, or can we make it go on forever? I dunno… *1994*

My enthusiasm has increased and I'm far more tolerant than before. I've dropped a lot of my old prejudices. But I'm not going to be growing a beard and long hair. Turning from a mod to a hippy? I can't go that far… *1994*

I still have this feeling that my time is yet to come, that I'm going to make something really great one day. Whether I will or not, I don't know. But that's part of what keeps me going. *1995*

I don't want to do the same things in life. I don't want to play the same sort of music all the time. I want to change, I need to change and find something different along the way. *1995*

I quite like the idea of being scattered. I don't like the prospect of some stone somewhere that people scratch their names on and piss against. I think I'd rather be scattered to the wind and forgotten about. There's a nice little church I've earmarked in Oxford. They can bung my ashes down there. *1995*

I still don't think I've done enough to warrant a biography.
Maybe when I'm older. I'm not sure whether or not I'd read it,
though. I was there, I know what happened, I don't need a book to
find out about my life. When I was at school, I read Hunter Davies'
Beatles biography, just because someone gave it to me. But I don't
have to read about John Lennon or Marvin Gaye or whoever to
understand them. I can tell what those people were like through
their music.

   I've hardly met anyone who I really admire. I'm not sure it's a
good idea. It's always a bit hit and miss, although I try not to expect
too much. I'm old enough now to realise that everyone has their good
and bad points. If I like someone's music, that's usually enough, but
you can't help but build up preconceptions. *1995*

I heard that song, 'White Line Fever' by the Burrito Brothers,
and I thought that was amazing. First of all I presumed it was about
coke – because Gram Parsons was well into that, wasn't he? – but
I realised it's about the road, how it keeps on going and you just keep
on burning up the miles on this journey. I think that's brilliant, that
idea of it never ending. *1996*